DELTORA QUEST

The Forests of Silence

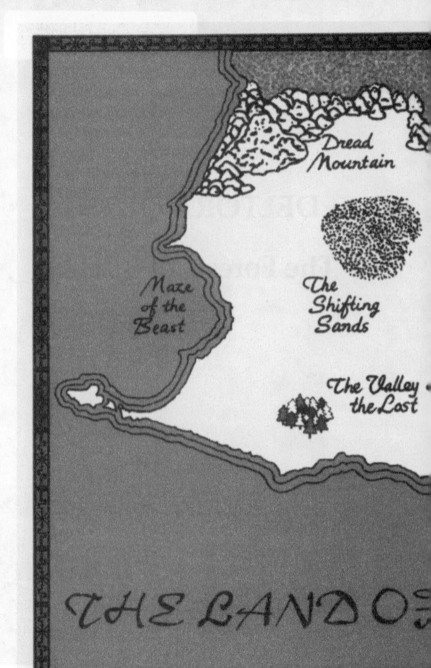

Dread
Mountain

Maze
of the
Beast

The
Shifting
Sands

The Valley
the Lost

THE LAND O

The Shadowlands

The Lake
of Tears

City
of the
Rats

The Forests
of Silence

Del

DELTORA

N
W · E
S

THE DELTORA QUEST SERIES

DELTORA QUEST

The Forests of Silence

Emily Rodda

A Scholastic Press
book
from
Scholastic Australia

LEXILE™ 750

Scholastic Press
345 Pacific Highway
Lindfield NSW 2070
an imprint of Scholastic Australia Pty Ltd (ABN 11 000 614 577)
PO Box 579,
Gosford NSW 2250.
www.scholastic.com.au

Part of the Scholastic Group
Sydney • Auckland • New York • Toronto • London • Mexico City
• New Delhi • Hong Kong • Buenos Aires • Puerto Rico

First published in 2000.
This edition published in 2006.
Text and graphics copyright © Emily Rodda, 2000.
Graphics by Kate Rowe.
Cover illustrations copyright © Scholastic Australia, 2000.
Cover illustrations by Marc McBride.

National Library of Australia Cataloguing-in-Publication entry
Rodda, Emily, 1948-.
    The forests of silence.
    For children.
    ISBN 9781865044095.
    1. Quests (Expeditions) - Juvenile fiction. I. Title. (Series : Rodda, Emily,
    1948- Deltora quest series ; 1).
A823.3

Typeset in Palatino.

Printed by McPherson's Printing Group, Victoria.

10 9 8 7 6 5 4 3 2 1   6789/0

CONTENTS

PART I: THE BELT OF DELTORA

1 - The King

Jarred stood unnoticed in the crowd thronging the great hall of the palace. He leaned against a marble pillar, blinking with tiredness and confusion.

It was midnight. He had been roused from his bed by shouts and bells. He had pulled on his clothes and joined the crowd of noble folk surging towards the hall.

'The king is dead,' the people were whispering. 'The young prince is to be crowned at once.'

Jarred could hardly take it in. The king of Deltora, with his long, plaited beard and his golden robes, had died of the mysterious fever that had kept him to his bed for the last few weeks. Never again would his deep, booming voice be heard in the hallways of the palace. Never again would he sit laughing in the feasting hall.

King Alton was dead, like his wife, the queen, before him. The fever had taken them both. And now . . .

'Now Endon will be king,' Jarred thought. He

shook his head, trying to make himself believe it. He and Endon had been friends since they were young children. But what a difference there was between them!

For Endon was the son of the king and queen, the prince of Deltora. And Jarred was the son of a trusted servant who had died in the king's service when Jarred was only four years old.

Jarred had been given to Endon as a companion, so that the young prince would not be lonely. They had grown up together, like brothers. Together they did their lessons in the schoolroom, teased the guards and persuaded the cooks in the kitchens to give them treats. Together they played in the vast green gardens.

The other children who lived in the palace—the sons and daughters of nobles and servants—kept to their own rooms and their own parts of the grounds. As was the palace custom, Jarred and Endon never even saw them, except in the great hall on feast days. But the two boys did what they could to entertain themselves.

They had a secret hiding place—a huge, hollow tree near the palace gates. There they hid from fussy old Min, their nursemaid, and Prandine, the king's chief advisor, a tall, thin, sour man they both disliked.

They practised archery together, playing a game called 'Aim High' where the first to shoot an arrow into the topmost fork of the hollow tree would win.

They invented a secret code and used it to pass messages, jokes and warnings to one another under the noses of their teachers, Min or Prandine.

Jarred would be hiding in the hollow tree, for example, because Min wanted him to take a dose of the fish-oil medicine he detested. Endon would walk by, and drop a note where he could reach it.

```
DEL ONEL O TELGEL O TELO TEL
HELE KEL ITEL CEL HELE NEL SEL
MEL I NELI SEL TELHEL E RELE
```

The message looked like nonsense, and no-one in the palace could guess the meaning if they picked up a note by accident. But the code was simple.

All you had to do to decode a message was write down all the letters in a line, leaving out 'EL' wherever it appeared.

DONOTGOTOTHEKITCHENSMINISTHERE

Then you divided the letters into words that made sense.

DO NOT GO TO THE KITCHENS. MIN IS THERE.

✳

As Endon and Jarred grew older there was less time for games. Their days were filled with tasks and duties.

Much of their time was spent learning the Rule—the thousands of laws and customs by which the royal family lived. The Rule governed their lives.

They sat—Endon patiently and Jarred not so patiently—while their long hair was plaited and twined with golden cord, according to the Rule. They spent hours learning to hammer red-hot metal into swords and shields. The first king of Deltora had been a blacksmith and it was part of the Rule that his art should be continued.

Each late afternoon they had a precious hour of free time. The only thing they were not allowed to do was to climb the high wall that surrounded the palace gardens, or go through the gates to the city beyond. For the prince of Deltora, like the king and queen, never mingled with the ordinary people. This was an important part of the Rule.

It was a part that Jarred was sometimes tempted to break. But Endon, quiet, dutiful and obedient, anxiously begged him not even to think of climbing the wall.

'It is forbidden,' he would say. 'And Prandine already fears that you are a bad influence on me, Jarred. He has told my father so. If you break the Rule you will be sent away. And I do not want that.'

Jarred did not want it, either. He knew he would miss Endon sorely. And where would he go if he had to leave the palace? It was the only home he had ever known. So he tamed his curiosity, and the city beyond the wall remained as much a mystery to him as it was to the prince.

The sound of the crystal trumpets broke into Jarred's thoughts. He turned, like everyone else, towards the back of the hall.

Endon was entering between two rows of royal guards in pale blue uniforms trimmed with gold.

Poor Endon, Jarred thought. He is grieving.

He wished that he could be beside his friend, to comfort him. But he had not been summoned. Instead, Chief Advisor Prandine stalked at Endon's right hand.

Jarred looked at Prandine with dislike. The advisor looked even taller and thinner than usual. He wore a long, purple robe and carried what looked like a box covered by a gold cloth. As he walked, his head poked forward so that he looked like a great bird of prey.

Endon's eyes were shadowed with sadness and he looked very small and pale in his stiff, silver jacket with its high, jewelled collar. But he held up his head bravely, as he had been taught to do.

All his life he had been trained for this moment. 'When I die, you will be king, my son,' his father had told him, so many times. 'Do not fail in your duty.'

'I will not fail, Father,' Endon would answer him obediently. 'I will do what is right, when the time comes.'

But neither Jarred nor Endon had thought the time would come so soon. The king was so strong and healthy that it had seemed that he would live forever.

Endon had reached the front of the hall now, and was mounting the steps to the platform. When he had reached the top, he turned and faced the sea of faces.

'He is so young,' a woman near Jarred breathed to her neighbour.

'Ssh,' the neighbour warned. 'He is the rightful heir.' As she spoke, she glanced nervously in Jarred's direction. Jarred did not recognise her face, but he realised that she knew him and feared he might tell Endon that her friend had been disloyal. He looked away quickly.

But now the crystal trumpets were sounding again and a low, excited murmuring had begun in the crowd.

Prandine had put his burden down on a small table beside the throne. He was sweeping the gold cloth aside to reveal a glass box. He was opening the box and taking out something that shone and glittered.

The magic Belt of Deltora. The crowd gave a hissing sigh, and Jarred, too, caught his breath. He had heard about the Belt since his earliest childhood, but he had never seen it before.

And here it was, in all its beauty and mystery— the ancient object that for thousands of years had kept Deltora safe from invasion by the evil Shadow Lord who ruled beyond the Mountains.

Hanging between Prandine's bony fingers, the Belt seemed as delicate as lace and the seven huge gems set along its length looked like beautiful decorations. But Jarred knew that the Belt was made of the strongest steel, and that each of the gems played its own special part in the magic that protected Deltora.

There was the topaz, symbol of faithfulness, gold as the setting sun. There was the amethyst, symbol of truth, purple as the violets that grew by the banks of the river Del. For purity and strength there was the diamond, clear and sparkling as ice. For honour there was the emerald, green as lush grass. There was the lapis-lazuli, the heavenly stone, midnight blue with pinpoints of silver like the night sky. There was the ruby for happiness, red as blood. And the opal, symbol of hope, sparkling with all the colours of the rainbow.

The crowd seemed to hold its breath as Prandine bent to loop the Belt around Endon's waist. The advisor's fingers fumbled with the fastening, and he was standing well back. He almost seems afraid, Jarred thought curiously. I wonder why?

Then, suddenly, the fastening snapped closed, and his question was answered. Prandine sprang backwards, there was a crackling sound and, at the same moment, the Belt seemed to explode with light.

The gems blazed like fire, lighting the hall with their rainbow brilliance. The people cried out and turned away, hiding their eyes.

Endon stood with his arms upraised, almost hidden by the flashing, darting light. No longer was he just a young boy with sad eyes. The magic Belt had recognised him as the true heir to the throne of Deltora. He, and he alone, could now use its mystery, magic and power.

But *will* Endon use them? Jarred thought suddenly. Did his father use them? Did his father ever do anything but follow rules laid down ages ago?

He watched as the fires of the gems slowly died to a winking glow. He watched as the young king took off the Belt and handed it to Prandine. He watched as Prandine, smiling now, put it back into its glass case.

Jarred knew what would happen to the Belt now. As the Rule stated, it would be carried back to the topmost room of the palace tower. The door of the room would be locked with three gold locks. Three guards in gold uniforms would be put outside the door.

And then . . . life would go on as before. Prandine and the other government officials would make all the real decisions affecting the kingdom.

The king would attend ceremonies and feasts, laugh at the clowns and acrobats in the great hall, practise archery and the blacksmith's art. He would sit for hours while his hair, and, one day, his beard, were plaited. He would sign endless documents, and stamp them with the ring that bore the royal seal. He would follow the Rule.

In a few years he would marry a young woman chosen for him by Prandine. A daughter of one of the noble families, who had also spent her life inside the palace walls. They would have a child, to take Endon's place when he died. And that child would also wear the Belt only once, before it was again locked away.

Now, for the first time in his life, Jarred wondered if this was a good idea. For the first time he wondered how and why the Belt was made. For the first time he began to doubt the wisdom of letting such a power for good remain idle in a tower room while the realm it was supposed to protect lay, unseen, outside high walls.

He slipped unnoticed out of the great hall and ran up the stairs to the palace library. This was another first for him. He had never loved study.

But there were things he needed to know. And the library was the only place he was likely to find them out.

2 - The Belt of Deltora

After hours of searching, Jarred finally found a book that he thought might help him. It was covered in faded pale blue cloth and the gold lettering on the outside had been worn away.

But the title inside was still very clear.

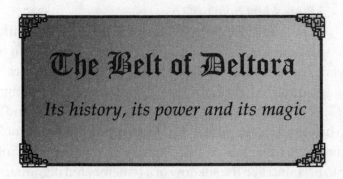

The Belt of Deltora

Its history, its power and its magic

This book was nothing like the splendid hand-painted

volumes that he and Endon read in the schoolroom. And nothing like the many other weighty books on the library shelves.

It was small, thin and very dusty. It had been tucked away in the library's darkest corner among piles of papers, as though someone had wanted it forgotten.

Jarred carried the old book carefully to a table. He planned to read it from beginning to end. His task might take him all night, but he did not expect to be disturbed. No-one would be looking for him. Endon would go straight from the great hall to the chapel where his father's body lay surrounded by candles. He would keep watch there alone till dawn, following the Rule.

Poor Endon, thought Jarred. It has only been a few days since he did the same for his mother. Now he is alone in the world, as I am. But at least we have each other. We are friends to the death. And I will protect him as best I can.

Protect him from what?

The question pierced his mind like a sharp knife. Why had he suddenly begun to fear for Endon? Who or what could threaten the all-powerful king of Deltora?

I am tired, thought Jarred. I am imagining things.

He shook his head impatiently and lit a fresh candle to brighten the darkness. But the memory of Prandine's thin smile as he locked the magic Belt away kept drifting into his mind like the shadow of a remembered nightmare. He frowned, lowered his head to the book, turned to the first page, and began to read.

✝   In ancient days, Deltora was divided into seven tribes. The tribes fought on their borders but otherwise stayed in their own place. Each had a gem from deep within the earth, a talisman with special powers.

✝   There came a time when the Enemy from the Shadowlands cast greedy eyes on Deltora. The tribes were divided, and singly none of them could repel the invader, who began to triumph.

✝   A hero called Adin rose from the ranks of the people. He was an ordinary man, a blacksmith who made swords and armour and shoes for horses. But he had been blessed with strength, courage and cleverness.

✝   One night, Adin dreamed of a special and splendid belt—seven steel medallions beaten to the thinness of silk and connected together with fine chain. To each medallion was fixed one of the tribal gems.

✝   Realising that the dream had been sent to him for a purpose, Adin worked in secret over many months to create a likeness of the belt he had been shown. Then he travelled around the kingdom to persuade each tribe to allow its talisman to be added to it.

✝   The tribes were at first suspicious and wary, but, one by one, desperate to save their land, they agreed. As each gem became part of the belt, its tribe grew stronger. But the people kept their strength secret, and bided their time.

✝   And when at last the belt was complete, Adin fastened it around his waist and it flashed like the sun. Then all the tribes united behind him to form a great army, and together they drove the Enemy from their land.

† And so Adin became the first king of the united tribes of Deltora and he ruled the land long and wisely. But he never forgot that he was a man of the people, and that their trust in him was the source of his power. Neither did he forget that the Enemy, though defeated, was not destroyed. He knew that the Enemy is clever and sly, and that to its anger and envy a thousand years is like the blink of an eye. So he wore the belt always, and never let it out of his sight . . .

Jarred read on and on, and the more he read, the more troubled he became. He had a pencil and some paper in his pocket, but he did not need to take notes. The words of the book seemed to be burning themselves into his brain. He was learning more than he expected. Not just about the Belt of Deltora, but about the Rule.

† The first to leave the belt aside was Adin's grandson, King Elstred, who in his middle years grew fat with good living and found the steel cut sadly into his belly. Elstred's chief advisor soothed his fears, saying that the belt need only be worn on great occasions. Elstred's daughter, Queen Adina, followed her father's ways, wearing the belt only five times in her reign. Her son, King Brandon, wore it only three times. And at last it became the custom for the belt only to be worn on the day the heir took the throne . . .

† At the urging of his chief advisor, King Brandon caused the Ralad builders to raise a great palace on the hill

at the centre of the city of Del. The royal family moved from the old blacksmith's forge to the palace, and over time it became the custom for them to remain within its walls, where no harm could come to them . . .

When Jarred closed the book at last, his heart was heavy. His candle had burned low and the first dawn light was showing at the window. He sat for a moment, thinking. Then he slipped the book into his shirt, and ran to seek Endon.

The chapel was below ground level, in a quiet corner of the palace. It was still and cold. The old king's body was lying on a raised marble platform in the centre, surrounded by candles. Endon was kneeling beside it, with his head bowed.

He looked up as Jarred burst in. His eyes were red with weeping. 'You should not be here, Jarred,' he whispered. 'It is against the Rule.'

'It is dawn,' Jarred panted. 'And I had to see you.'

Endon stood up stiffly and came over to him. 'What is it?' he asked in a low voice.

Jarred's head was full of everything he had read. The words came tumbling out of him. 'Endon, you should wear the Belt of Deltora always, as the ancient kings and queens did.'

Endon stared at him in puzzlement.

'Come!' Jarred urged, taking his arm. 'Let us go and get it now.'

13

But Endon held back, shaking his head. 'You know I cannot do that, Jarred. The Rule—'

Jarred stamped his foot with impatience. 'Forget the Rule! It is just a collection of traditions that have grown up over the years and been made law by the chief advisors. It is dangerous, Endon! Because of it, every new ruler of Deltora has been more powerless than the one before. This must stop—with you! You must get the Belt and put it on. Then you must come with me outside the palace gates.'

He was speaking too fast and too wildly. By now Endon was frowning, backing away from him. 'You are ill, my friend,' he was whispering nervously. 'Or you have been dreaming.'

'No!' Jarred insisted, following him. 'It is you who are living in a dream. You must see how things are outside the palace—in the city and beyond.'

'I see the city, Jarred,' argued Endon. 'I look out at it from my window every day. It is beautiful.'

'But you do not talk to the people. You do not walk among them!'

'Of course I do not! That is forbidden by the Rule!' Endon gasped. 'But I know that all is well.'

'You know nothing, except what you are told by Prandine!' shouted Jarred.

'And is that not enough?' The cold voice cut through the air like sharp steel.

3 - Escape

Startled, Endon and Jarred spun around. Prandine was standing in the doorway. His eyes, fixed on Jarred, glittered with hatred.

'How dare you tempt the king to turn from his duty and the Rule, servant boy?' he hissed, striding into the chapel. 'You have always been jealous of him. And now you seek to destroy him. Traitor!'

'No!' exclaimed Jarred. He turned again to Endon. 'Believe me!' he begged. 'I have only your good at heart.' But Endon shrank away from him, horrified.

Jarred plunged his hand into his shirt to get the book—to show it to Endon, prove to him that he had good reason for what he said.

'Beware, your majesty! He has a knife!' shouted Prandine, leaping forward and sweeping Endon under his cloak as if to protect him. He raised his voice to a shriek. 'Murderer! Traitor! Guards! Guards!'

For a single moment Jarred stood frozen. Then he heard bells of warning ringing. He heard shouts of alarm and heavy feet thudding towards the chapel. He saw Prandine's mocking, triumphant smile. He realised that Prandine had been given the chance he had been waiting for—the chance to rid himself of Jarred for good.

Jarred knew that if he valued his life he would have to flee. Pushing Prandine aside, he ran like the wind from the chapel, up the stairs and to the back of the palace. He plunged into the huge, dim kitchens where the cooks were just beginning to light the fires in the great stoves. Behind him he could hear the shouts of the guards: 'Traitor! Stop him! Stop him!'

But the cooks did not try to stop Jarred. How could they think that he was the one the guards were pursuing? He was the young king's friend, and they had known him all his life. So they only watched as Jarred tore open the kitchen door and ran outside.

The grounds were deserted, except for a ragged old man tipping food scraps into a horse-drawn cart. He took no notice as Jarred plunged under the cover of the thick bushes that grew against the palace walls.

Keeping low, Jarred crawled through the bushes to the front of the palace. Then he ran, dodging and weaving, till he reached the tree near the gates where so often he and Endon had hidden from Min in the old days.

He crept into the tree's hollow and huddled there, panting. He knew that the guards would surely find him in the end. Perhaps Endon would even tell them where to look. And when they found him they would kill him. Of that he had no doubt.

He cursed himself for being impatient. For scaring Endon with wild talk while he was still confused, tired and grieving. For playing into Prandine's hands.

There was a squeaking, rattling sound not far away. Peering cautiously out of his hollow, Jarred saw the rubbish cart trundling around the side of the palace, heading for the gates. The old man sat at the front, urging his tired horse on with sad shakes of the reins.

Jarred's heart leapt. Perhaps there was a chance of escape from the palace after all! But how could he run away, leaving Endon alone and unprotected? He was sure now that Prandine was evil.

If you stay, you will die. And then you will never be able to help Endon. Never.

The thought brought him to his senses. He pulled out his pencil and paper and scrawled a note.

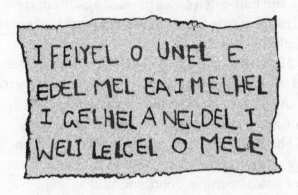

I FEIYEL O UNEL E
EDEL MEL EA I MELHEL
I GELHEL A NELDEL I
WELI LELCEL O MELE

He tucked the note into a hole in the tree's trunk, wondering if his friend would ever see it. Perhaps Endon, believing what Prandine said of him, would never come to this place again.

But he had done what he could, and the cart was coming closer. Soon it would pass under the tree. That would be his chance.

As he had done so many times before, he climbed up through the hollow trunk of the tree and squeezed out of the hole that gaped just above its lowest branch.

From here he could see that there were guards everywhere. But he was used to hiding. He lay on his stomach, flattening himself against the branch, being careful not to make it sway.

The rubbish cart was underneath him now. He waited until just the right moment then dropped lightly onto the back, burrowing quickly into the sticky mess of scraps until he was completely covered.

Bread crusts, apple peel, mouldy cheese, gnawed bones and half-eaten cakes pressed against his face. The smell nearly made him choke. He screwed his eyes shut and held his breath.

He could hear the sound of the horse's feet. He could hear the distant shouting of the guards searching for him. And at last he could hear the sound of the first pair of great wooden gates creaking open.

His heart thudded as the cart trundled on. Then he heard the gates closing behind him and the second pair of gates opening. Soon, soon . . .

The cart moved on, swaying and jolting. With a creak the second pair of gates slammed shut. And then Jarred knew that, for the first time in his life, he was outside the palace walls. The cart was trundling down the hill, now. Soon he would actually be in the beautiful city he had seen so often from his window.

He had to look. His curiosity was too great. Slowly he wriggled until his eyes and nose were above the mound of scraps.

He was facing back towards the palace. He could see the wall, and the gates. He could see the top of the hollow. But—Jarred squinted in puzzlement—why could he not see the turrets of the palace, or the tops of the other trees in the gardens? Above the wall there was only shining mist.

He thought his eyes were at fault, and rubbed them. But the mist did not disappear.

Confused, he turned his head to look down towards the city. And his shock, dismay and horror were so great that he almost cried out. For instead of beauty he saw ruin.

The fine buildings were crumbling. The roads were filled with holes. The grain fields were brown and choked with weeds. The trees were stunted and bent. Waiting at the bottom of the hill was a crowd of thin, ragged people carrying baskets and bags.

Jarred began struggling to free himself from the rubbish. In his confusion he no longer cared if the driver of the cart heard him or not, but the old man did not look around. Jarred realised that he was deaf. Unable to speak, too, no doubt, for he had not uttered a single word, even to the horse.

Jarred leapt from the back of the cart and rolled into a ditch at the side of the road. He lay, watching, as the cart moved on to the bottom of the hill and stopped. The old man sat staring ahead of him while the ragged people swarmed onto the pile of rubbish. Jarred saw them fighting each other for the scraps from the palace tables, stuffing old bones, crusts and vegetable peelings into their baskets and into their mouths.

They were starving.

Sick at heart, Jarred looked back at the palace. From here he could just see the tips of the palace turrets, rising above the shimmering mist.

Endon might be looking from his window at this moment, staring down at the city. He would be seeing peace, beauty and plenty. He would be seeing a lie. A lie created by pictures on a misty screen.

For how many years had this evil magic blinded the eyes of the kings and queens of Deltora? And who had created it?

Words from the book came to Jarred's mind. He shuddered with dread.

. . . *the Enemy is clever and sly, and to its anger and envy a thousand years is like the blink of an eye.*

The Shadow Lord was stirring.

4 - The Forge

Afterwards, Jarred could barely remember scrambling from the ditch. He could not remember stumbling through the tangled weeds and thorny bushes beyond the road. He did not know what guided him to the blacksmith's forge, where at last he fell, fainting, to the ground.

Perhaps he saw the glow of the fire. Perhaps he heard the hammer beating on the red-hot metal, and the sound reminded him of his lessons with Endon. Or perhaps the spirit of Adin was looking after him. For Crian the blacksmith, stubborn and fearless, was perhaps the only man in Del who would have taken him in.

Crian roused him and helped him into the small house behind the forge. At his call, a sweet-faced girl came running. Her eyes were full of questions, but she was silent as she helped Crian give Jarred water and bread and bathe his cuts and scratches. They took his filthy, torn clothes, gave him a long, plain nightshirt and tucked him into a narrow bed.

Then Jarred slept.

When he woke, the great hammer was ringing on metal once more, the girl was singing in the kitchen and the sun was setting. He had slept the day through.

At the end of his bed he found a set of clothes. He pulled them on, tidied the bed and crept outside.

He found Crian at work in the forge. The old man turned and looked at him without speaking.

'I thank you for your kindness with all my heart,' Jarred said awkwardly. 'I will leave now, for I do not want to cause you trouble. But I beg you not to say I was here if the palace guards come searching. They will tell you I tried to kill the new king. But I did not do it.'

'So much the worse,' the old man answered grimly, returning to his work. 'Many in Del would thank you if you had.'

Jarred caught his breath. So this was how things were. The king was not loved, but hated. And no wonder. As far as his people knew, he lived in luxury behind his high walls while they suffered. They did not understand that he had no idea of their trouble.

'The guards will not come,' the old man said, without turning around. 'I threw your clothes over a cliff into the sea and watched as they found them. They think that you are drowned.'

Jarred did not know what to say. He saw that Crian had finished the horseshoe he had been hammering.

Without thinking, he picked up the heavy tongs beside the forge and stepped forward. Crian glanced at him in surprise, but let him pick up the shoe and dip it into the barrel of water standing ready. The water hissed and bubbled as the iron cooled.

'You have done this work before,' the old man murmured.

Jarred nodded. 'A little,' he said. Carefully, he lifted the horseshoe from the water and laid it aside.

'I am old,' Crian said, watching him. 'My son, whose clothes you are wearing now, was killed three years ago. His dear wife died before him, when their child was born. I have only that child, Anna, now. We live simply, but there is always food on the table. And will be, while I keep my strength.'

He glanced down at Jarred's hands—soft and white, with long, rounded nails. 'You could stay here, boy,' he said. 'But you would have to work hard to earn your keep. Could you do it?'

'I could,' said Jarred strongly.

Nothing would please him more than to stay. He liked the old blacksmith. He liked the calm, sweet-faced Anna. Here, too, he would be close to the palace. He could do nothing for Endon now except to keep watch. But he had vowed that this he would do.

Prandine thought he was dead. But he would be unlikely to tell Endon so. It would suit his purpose better to let the king think Jarred was still alive, and dangerous. If he feared for his life, Endon would be even more willing to do exactly as he was told.

But one day Endon may realise that after all I was right, thought Jarred. One day he may call me. And if ever that happens, I will be ready.

So, it was settled. Jarred took shears and cut off the long plaits of hair that marked him so plainly as coming from the palace. And after that, every day, he worked in the forge.

He already knew how to hammer hot iron and steel to make fine swords and shields. Now he had to learn to make simpler things, like horseshoes, axes and blades for ploughs. But this he did quickly, and as his muscles hardened and his soft hands grew tough he took over more and more of the blacksmith's work.

The forge was busy, but still Crian and Anna were poor. Jarred soon discovered that this was because most of the people in Del were even poorer, and could pay little for the work the blacksmith did for them. Some, indeed, could give nothing. And these Crian would help all the same, saying, 'Pay me when you can.'

By the second day, Jarred had realised with a sinking heart that everything he and Endon had been taught about life outside the palace had been a lie. The city was a place of hunger, illness and struggle. Beyond its walls, strange, terrible beasts and bands of robbers prowled. For many years no news had come from the towns and villages scattered through the countryside.

Many people were weak with hunger. Yet it was said that in the dead of night heavily guarded carts piled high with food and drink trundled into the city and up to the palace gates. No-one knew where the carts came from.

'Somewhere far away, in any case,' Crian muttered, as they sat by the fire on the second night. 'Such luxuries could not be found here.'

'It is said that Deltora was once a land of peace and plenty,' Anna added. 'But that was a long time ago.'

'The new king knows nothing of this!' Jarred cried. 'Neither did the old king. You should have told him—'

'*Told* him?' Crian growled angrily. 'We told him time and again!' He swung around in his chair and pulled an old tin box from the shelf. He thrust the box at Jarred. 'Open it!' he ordered.

Jarred lifted the lid of the box. Inside were many small rolls of parchment edged with gold. Confused, he picked out one of the rolls and straightened it.

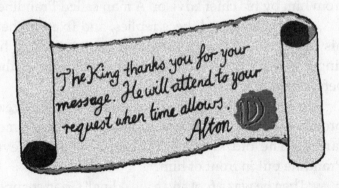

The King thanks you for your message. He will attend to your request when time allows.
Alton

Frowning, Jarred thrust the parchment back into the box and picked out another. It was exactly the same.

And so was the next he looked at, and the next. The only difference in the fourth was that it spoke of 'The Queen' instead of 'The King' and was signed, 'Lilia'. Queen Lilia had been Alton's mother, Jarred remembered.

He scrabbled through the parchments. There were hundreds of them, all stamped with the royal seal. Some were much older than others, signed with royal names he remembered from his history lessons.

'They are all the same,' Crian said, watching him reading one after the other. 'The only difference between them is the name at the bottom. For centuries messages have been sent to the palace, begging for help. And these accursed parchments are all the people have ever received in return. Nothing has ever been done. Nothing!'

Jarred's throat tightened with pain and anger. 'King Alton, at least, never received your messages, Crian,' he said, as calmly as he could. 'I think they were kept from him by his chief advisor. A man called Prandine.'

'The king signed these replies, and fixed to them his royal seal,' Crian pointed out coldly, flicking his finger at the box. 'As did his mother and grandfather before him.'

'It is the Rule—the custom—that the chief advisor prepares all replies for the king to sign,' exclaimed Jarred. 'The old king signed and sealed whatever Prandine put in front of him.'

'Then he was a fool and a weakling!' Crian snapped back. 'As no doubt his son is also! Endon will be as useless to us as his father.' He shook his head. 'I fear for

Deltora,' he muttered. 'We are now so weak that should invasion come from the Shadowlands we could do nothing to protect ourselves.'

'The Shadow Lord will not invade, Grandfather,' Anna soothed. 'Not while the Belt of Deltora protects us. And our king guards the Belt. That, at least, he does for us.'

Jarred felt a chill of fear. But he could not bring himself to tell Anna that she was wrong. If she found out that the king did not wear the Belt, but let it be shut away, under the care of others, she would lose the last of her hope.

'Oh, Endon,' he thought, as he went to bed that night. 'I cannot reach you unless you wish it. You are too well guarded. But you can reach me. Go to the hollow tree. Read my note. Send the signal.'

From that time on, before he started work each morning, Jarred looked up at the tree rising against the misty cloud on the hill. He would look carefully, searching for the glint of the king's golden arrow at the top. The signal that Endon needed him.

But it was a long, long time before the signal came. And by then it was too late.

5 - The Enemy Strikes

Years passed and life went on. Jarred and Anna married. Then old Crian died and Jarred took his place as blacksmith.

Sometimes Jarred almost forgot that he had ever had another life. It was as if his time at the palace had been a dream. But still, every dawn, he looked up to the tree on the hill. And still he often read the small book he had found in the palace library. Then he feared for what the future might hold. He feared for his beloved Anna and the child they were expecting. He feared for himself, for Endon and for the whole of Deltora.

One night, exactly seven years after the night Endon was crowned, Jarred tossed restlessly in his bed.

'It is nearly daybreak and you have not slept, Jarred,' Anna said gently, at last. 'What is troubling you?'

'I do not know, dear heart,' Jarred murmured. 'But I cannot rest.'

'Perhaps the room is too warm,' she said, climbing out of bed. 'I will open the window a little more.'

She had pulled the curtains aside and was reaching for the window fastening when suddenly she screamed and jumped back.

Jarred leapt up and ran to her.

'There!' Anna exclaimed, pointing, as he put his arm around her. 'Oh, Jarred, what are they?'

Jarred stared through the window and caught his breath. In the sky above the palace on the hill, monstrous shapes were wheeling and circling.

It was still too dark to see them clearly. But there was no doubt that they were huge birds. There were seven. Their necks were long. Their great, hooked beaks were cruel. Their mighty wings flapped clumsily but strongly, beating at the air. As Jarred watched, they swooped, rose again and then separated, flying off swiftly in different directions.

A name came to him. A name from the schoolroom of his past.

'Ak-Baba,' he hissed. His arm tightened around Anna's shoulders.

She turned to him, her eyes wide and frightened.

'Ak-Baba,' he repeated slowly, still staring at the palace. 'Great birds that eat dead flesh and live for a thousand years. Seven of them serve the Shadow Lord.'

'Why are they here?' Anna whispered.

'I do not know. But I fear—' Jarred broke off abruptly and leaned forward. He had seen something glinting brightly in the first feeble rays of the sun.

For a moment he stood motionless. Then he turned to Anna, his face grim and pale.

'Endon's arrow is in the tree,' he said. 'The call has come.'

✳

In moments Jarred had dressed and run from the house behind the forge. He hurried up the hill to the palace, his mind racing.

How was he to reach Endon? If he climbed the wall, the guards inside would certainly see him. He would be hit by a dozen arrows before he reached the ground. The cart that collected the food scraps would be no use to him. Prandine must have guessed that Jarred had used it to escape, because it was no longer permitted to enter the palace. These days it waited between the two sets of gates while guards loaded it with sacks.

Endon himself is the only one who can help me, Jarred thought, as he ran. Perhaps he will be watching for me, waiting for me . . .

But as he slowed, panting, in sight of the palace gates, he could see that they were firmly closed and the road outside was deserted.

Jarred moved closer, his spine prickling. The long grass that ringed the palace walls whispered in the breeze of dawn. He could be walking into a trap. Perhaps at any moment guards would spring from their hiding places in the grass and lay hands on him. Perhaps Endon had at last decided to betray him to Prandine.

His feet brushed something lying in the dust of the road. He looked down and saw a child's wooden arrow. A small piece of paper had been rolled around the arrow's shaft and tied there.

His heart beating hard, Jarred picked up the arrow and pulled away the paper. But as he flattened it out and looked at it, his excitement died.

It was just a child's drawing. Some palace child had been playing a game, practising shooting arrows over the wall as he and Endon once had done.

Jarred screwed up the paper in disgust and threw it to the ground. He looked around again at the closed gates, the empty road. Still there was no movement, no sign. There was nothing but the wooden arrow lying in the dust and the little ball of paper rolling slowly away from him, driven by the breeze. He stared at it, and the foolish little rhyme came back to him.

Strange, he thought idly. That rhyme sounds almost like a set of instructions. Instructions that a small child could chant and remember.

An idea seized him. He ran after the paper and snatched it up again. He smoothed out the creases and looked at it closely, this time seeing two things that he had overlooked before. The paper was yellowed with age. And the writing, though childish, was strangely familiar.

This is the way Endon used to print when he was small, he thought in wonder. And Endon drew the picture, too. I am sure of it!

Suddenly he realised what must have happened. Endon had had little time. Yet he had wanted to send Jarred a message. So he had snatched up one of his old childhood drawings and sent it over the wall. He had used a child's wooden arrow so that the guards would take no notice if they saw it lying on the road.

And if Jarred was right, Endon had not chosen just any drawing. This one had a special meaning for him. Why else would he have kept it?

Wake the bear,
Do not fear . . .

Jarred waited no longer. With the paper clutched

in his hand he left the road and moved left, following the wall.

The road was out of sight by the time he found what he was searching for. Even overgrown with long grass and shadowed by a clump of straggly bushes, the shape of the huge rock was clear. It really did look exactly like a sleeping animal.

Jarred forced his way through the undergrowth to the rock. He saw that at one end, where the bear's nose rested on its paws, the grass grew less strongly than it did anywhere else. Why would that be? Unless . . .

'Time to wake up, old bear,' Jarred muttered aloud. He ran to the place, threw himself to his knees and began pulling at the weak grass. It came away easily and as he scrabbled in the earth beneath it Jarred realised with a wave of relief that he had been right. There was only a thin layer of soil here. Beneath it was a large, round metal plate.

It took only moments for his powerful hands to uncover the plate completely and pull it aside. A dark hole was revealed. Its walls were lined with stone. In wonder, Jarred realised that he had found the entrance to a tunnel.

Scurry, mouse,
Into your house . . .

He knew what he must do. He lay flat on his stomach and wriggled into the hole, pulling himself forward on his elbows until the space broadened and his way became easier.

So now the mouse is in the mouse hole, he thought grimly, as he crawled along in the darkness. Let us hope that no cat is waiting at the other end.

For a short time the tunnel sloped downwards, then it became more level and Jarred realised that he was moving through the centre of the hill. The air was still, the walls around him were ancient stone and the blackness was complete. He crawled on, losing all track of time.

At last the tunnel ended in a set of steep stone steps that led upwards. His heart thudding, Jarred began to climb blindly. He had to feel his way—up, up, one step at a time. Then, without warning, the top of his head hit hard stone. With a shock he realised that the way above was blocked. He could go no further.

Hot panic flared in him. Had this been a trap after all? Were guards even now creeping through the tunnel after him, knowing that they would find him cowering here, without hope of escape?

Then, through the confusion of his thoughts, he remembered.

Lift the lid,
Be glad you did.

The panic died. Jarred stretched up his arms, pushed firmly and felt the stone above his head move. He pushed harder, then staggered and nearly fell as with a grating sound the stone moved smoothly aside.

He climbed the last few steps and crawled out of blackness into soft, flickering light.

'Who are you?' barked a deep, angry voice.

A tall, shimmering figure was looming over him. Jarred blinked up at it. After being so long in darkness, his eyes were watering, dazzled by the light. 'My name is Jarred,' he cried. 'Stay back!'

He scrambled to his feet, blindly feeling for his sword.

Then, suddenly, with a rustle of rich silk and the clinking of golden ornaments, the figure was falling to its knees before him.

'Oh, Jarred, how could I not have known you?' the voice cried. 'For the sake of our old friendship, I beg you to forgive the past. You are the only one I can trust. Please help us!'

And only then did Jarred realise that the man at his feet was Endon.

6 - Friends to the Death

With a shaky laugh, Jarred bent to raise the kneeling king. 'Endon! I did not know you either! Get up, for mercy's sake!'

As he stared, his eyes slowly adjusting to the light, he thought that it was no wonder he had not recognised his old friend.

The slim, solemn boy he had left behind him seven years ago had become a man. Endon had grown as tall and broad-shouldered as Jarred himself. His stiff robes and high collar were encrusted with tiny gems that glittered in the light. His eyes were outlined with black and his eyelids coloured blue, in the palace fashion. His long hair and beard were plaited and twined with gold. He smelt of perfume and spices. To Jarred, who had been so long away from the palace and its ways, he made a strange, awesome picture.

Jarred realised that Endon was staring at him, too,

and suddenly became aware of his workman's clothes, his thick boots, his rough beard and untidy hair. He felt clumsy and awkward and to hide this he turned away.

As he did, he at last realised where he was. He was in the chapel. One of the marble tiles that surrounded the raised platform in the centre had been pushed aside, and a dark hole gaped where it had lain.

'The tunnel through the hill is known only to the royal family, and is only to be used in times of great danger,' he heard Endon say softly. 'King Brandon caused it to be made when the palace was built. My father taught me of it when I was very young, as he had been taught in his time—in words that even a small child would remember. There is a rhyme for entering the palace, and a rhyme for leaving it. It is a dark secret. Even the chief advisors have never known of it.'

Jarred did not reply. He had raised his eyes to the platform and seen what was lying there. It was the body of an old woman. Her work-worn hands were folded on her chest. Her wrinkled face was peaceful in the flickering light of the candles that surrounded her.

'Min!' he whispered. His eyes burned with sudden tears as he looked at the old nurse who had cared for him through his childhood. He had not seen her for many years, but he had thought of her often. It was hard to believe that she was dead.

'She had a grown-up son, you know,' Endon murmured. 'He lived in the palace, but I never met him. I asked for him, when I heard she had died. They told

37

me he had run away—escaped through the gates during the feast. He was afraid, Jarred. Min must have told him what she heard. He knew she had been killed . . .'

'Killed?' gasped Jarred. 'But—'

Endon's face was twisted with sorrow. 'She came to me in my chamber. I was about to leave for the feast celebrating my seven years as king,' he muttered. 'She was troubled. She had been working in her sewing room, and had overheard whisperings outside that frightened her. She told me that there were enemies within the palace, and that some great evil was to strike this night.'

He bowed his head. 'I would not listen to her. I thought she had fallen asleep over her work, and dreamed. I smiled at her fears and sent her away. And within the hour, she was dead. She had fallen from the top of the stairs to the hall below. They said it was an accident. But . . .'

'But you do not think so,' Jarred finished for him, looking sadly at Min's still, pale face. 'You think she was killed because of what she knew.'

'Yes,' said Endon in a low voice. 'And my wife thinks it, too.'

Jarred glanced at him. 'You are married, then,' he said. 'I, too.'

Endon half-smiled. 'That is good,' he murmured politely. 'I hope that you are as happy in your marriage as I am in mine. My wife, the Queen, is called Sharn. We had never spoken to one another before our wedding day, as is the Rule, but she grows more dear to me with every year that passes. Our first child will be born at summer's end.'

'And ours in the early autumn,' said Jarred.

There was a moment's silence as each of them thought of the changes that seven years had brought. Then Endon looked straight into Jarred's eyes. 'It is good to see you again, my friend,' he said softly. 'I have been cruelly punished for believing that you could betray me. I have missed you sorely.'

And suddenly all the strangeness between them melted away. Jarred thrust out his hand and clasped Endon's warmly. 'Friends to the death we were as boys, and friends to the death we will always be,' he said. 'You must have always known this in your heart, Endon, because you sent for me when trouble came. I wish only that the summons had been sooner. I fear we have little time.'

'Then Min was right,' Endon whispered. 'There is evil here.'

'There has been evil here for a long time,' said Jarred. 'And now—'

Both of them swung around, their hands on their swords, as they heard the door behind them click open.

'Endon, it is past dawn,' a voice called softly.

'Sharn!' exclaimed Endon. He ran to meet the pretty young woman who was slipping into the chapel. She was as richly robed as he, and her glossy hair was twisted high on her head. There were deep shadows under her eyes as if she had kept watch all night.

She gasped and shrank back as she saw Jarred.

'Do not be afraid, Sharn,' Endon said gently. 'It is only Jarred.'

'Jarred! You came!' she exclaimed, her tired face breaking into a relieved smile.

'I did,' nodded Jarred. 'And I will do what I can to help you fight the trouble that has come to our land. But we must act quickly. We must go at once to the tower, so that Endon can reclaim the Belt of Deltora.'

Endon stared at him, white-faced. 'Jarred, I—I cannot,' he stammered. 'The Rule—'

'Forget the Rule, Endon!' Jarred hissed, striding towards the door. 'I told you this once and you would not listen to me. Do not make the mistake a second time. The Belt is Deltora's only protection. The people depend upon you to guard it. And I think that it is in danger. Grave danger.'

As Endon stood motionless, still hesitating, Sharn put her arm through his. 'You are the King, Endon,' she said quietly. 'Your duty to Deltora is far greater than your duty to obey the Rule. Let us go together to the tower.'

And, at last, Endon nodded. 'Very well,' he said. 'We will go. Together.'

❋

They ran up the great stairs—past the first floor, the second, the third and on towards the tower room. They took care to move quietly, but they saw no-one. It was still very early, and though the cooks had begun to move around in the kitchens downstairs, few others in the palace were stirring.

By the time they reached the last flight of stairs, Jarred had begun to think that all was going to be well. He climbed eagerly, with Endon and Sharn close behind him. He reached the top—then stopped abruptly.

The tower room door was gaping open, its three gold locks broken. On the floor outside, the three guards lay dead where they had fallen, their swords still clutched in their hands.

Jarred heard a sobbing gasp behind him. Then Endon had run past him into the tower room. There was a single, anguished cry. Then silence.

Jarred's heart seemed to turn over in his chest. Slowly he and Sharn followed the king.

The small, round room was very still and a foul smell hung in the air. The sky outside the open windows was filled with angry red light as the newly risen sun glared through a smothering blanket of cloud. The glass case which sheltered the Belt of Deltora had been shattered into a thousand pieces.

Endon was on his knees among the glittering fragments. The Belt—or what remained of it—lay on the floor in front of him. He picked it up. It hung limply between his hands—a tangled, useless chain of grey steel. Its medallions were torn and twisted. The seven gems were gone.

7 - Treachery

With a cry, Sharn hurried to her husband's side, gently helping him to rise. He stood, swaying, the empty, ruined Belt clutched in his hands. Dull despair settled over Jarred. What he had feared had come to pass. The enemy had triumphed.

There was a low, mocking laugh behind him. Prandine was standing in the doorway. In his long, black robe he looked as tall and bony as ever, but it was as if a mask had fallen from his face. The grave, serious expression had gone. Now, greed and triumph lit his eyes and cruelty twisted his thin mouth.

'So, Jarred, you have risen from the dead to try to interfere once more,' he snarled. 'But you are too late. Soon, very soon, Deltora will bow beneath my Lord's shadow.'

Wild anger surged through Jarred. He lunged forward, his sword aimed at Prandine's heart. In an instant, the sword burned white hot. He dropped it with a cry of agony, his hand seared and blistered.

'You were a fool to come here,' spat Prandine. 'If you had not, I would have gone on believing you safely dead. Now you are doomed, like your idiot king, his little painted doll bride and the brat she carries.'

From his robe he drew a long, thin dagger, its wicked tip glowing sickly green.

Jarred backed away from him, fighting back the pain from his injured hand, trying desperately to think. He had no wish to die, but he knew that at all costs he must save Endon, Sharn and their unborn child, the heir to the throne of Deltora.

'We are too many for you, Prandine,' he said loudly. 'While you struggle with one, the others can escape.' He wondered if Prandine would realise that this was not just a challenge to him, but a message for Endon. *While I distract him, take Sharn and run!*

But Prandine was laughing again, kicking the door shut behind him. 'There will be no struggle,' he jeered, moving forward. 'The poison on this blade is deadly. One tiny scratch and the end comes quickly. As it did for your mother and father, King Endon.'

'Murderer! Traitor!' breathed Endon, pushing Sharn behind him. 'You have betrayed your king, and your land.'

'This is not my land,' sneered Prandine. 'My loyalty, like the loyalty of the chief advisors before me, has always been to another place and to a far greater master.'

He looked at Endon with contempt. 'You are the last in a line of royal buffoons, King Endon. Little by little we robbed your family of power until you were nothing but puppets moving as we pulled the strings. And then, at last, the time was right to take your last protection from you.'

He pointed a bony finger at the tangled chain in Endon's hands. 'Finally, the blacksmith Adin's accursed work has been undone. The Belt of Deltora is no more.'

'The gems cannot be destroyed,' Endon said through pale lips. 'And it is death to take them beyond Deltora's borders.'

Prandine smiled cruelly. 'The gems have been scattered far and wide, hidden where no-one would dare to find them. And when you and your unborn brat are dead, finding them would be no use in any case.'

The room darkened and thunder growled outside the tower. Prandine's eyes glowed with triumph. 'The Shadow Lord comes,' he hissed.

Cowering against the wall, Sharn moaned softly. Then she seemed to hear something. She sidled to the open window and looked out—not up to the black sky, but down, to the ground below the tower. The next moment she had jumped back, covering her mouth with her hand as if to smother a shriek.

'What is it?' snarled Prandine, suddenly alert.

Sharn shook her head. 'Nothing,' she stammered. 'I was mistaken. There is no-one there.'

Oh, Sharn, even a child could tell that you are lying!

thought Jarred desperately. Thanks to you, whoever has come to help us is doomed.

'Stay where you are or she dies at once!' barked Prandine to the two men as he crossed the room.

Sharn shrank away from him as he reached her. 'Do not look out! There is no-one there!' she cried again.

'So you say,' Prandine sneered. He thrust his head and shoulders out of the open window.

And in the next instant Sharn had crouched behind him, thrown her arms around his knees, jerked his legs back and upwards and tipped him over the sill.

Jarred and Endon, frozen with shock, listened to their enemy's screams as he plunged to the hard earth far below. They both stared, astounded, at the small figure turning from the window to face them.

'Often, in the great hall, I have watched little clowns upset big ones from below,' Sharn said calmly. 'I did not see why the trick should not work for me.'

'What—what did you see from the window?' Jarred stammered.

'Nothing. As I told him. But I knew he would not trust my word.' Sharn tossed her head. 'And I knew he would lean out. Why should he fear a little painted doll like me?'

Jarred gazed at her in frank admiration, then turned to Endon. 'You are as fortunate in your bride as I am in mine,' he said.

Endon nodded slowly. He seemed dazed.

Thunder growled outside, threatening as an angry

beast. Black clouds edged with scarlet were tumbling towards the tower.

'We must hurry to the tunnel,' Jarred said urgently. 'Come quickly!'

✳

The palace was echoing with frightened voices as they ran down the stairs. The people were waking to darkness and terror.

'I have brought them to this,' moaned Endon, as they reached the chapel door. 'How can I leave them?'

'You have no choice, Endon,' panted Jarred. 'Your family must survive or Deltora will be lost to the Shadow Lord forever.'

He pushed Endon and Sharn into the chapel and closed the door behind them. 'We will go straight to the forge,' he said, hurrying towards the tunnel entrance. 'There we will think what we should do.'

'We must flee the city, and find a place to hide,' said Sharn.

But Endon's hands tightened on the tangled handful of steel that had once been the Belt of Deltora.

'I cannot run and hide!' he burst out. 'I must find the gems and restore them to the Belt. Without them I am helpless and Deltora is doomed.'

Glancing at Sharn's worried face, Jarred took his friend's arm. 'The gems must be found, but you cannot be the one to find them, Endon,' he said firmly. 'The Shadow Lord will be searching for you. You must stay in hiding, and wait.'

'But what if I die before the Belt is whole again?' Endon argued desperately. 'It will only recognise Adin's true heir. It will only shine for me!'

Jarred opened his mouth to speak, then thought better of it. Soon enough Endon would realise for himself that he had lost the last trust his people had in him. The Belt of Deltora would never shine for him again.

But Sharn had moved quietly to her husband's side. 'Do not forget, my dear,' she murmured. 'Our child will also be Adin's heir.'

Endon stared at her, open-mouthed. She lifted her chin proudly.

'If the Shadow Lord can be patient, so can we,' she said. 'We will hide ourselves away from him for now. But it will not be for fear of our own lives, as he will think. It will be to keep our child safe, and to prepare for the future.'

She stroked his arm lovingly. 'Years will pass and we may die, Endon,' she said. 'But our child will live after us, to reclaim the kingdom and lift this evil from our land.'

Jarred's heart swelled at her courage. And at that moment he himself found the courage to face what he must do.

Endon had gathered Sharn close to him. 'You are indeed a precious gift,' he was murmuring. 'But you do not understand. Without the Belt our child cannot defeat the Shadow Lord. The gems—'

'One day the gems will be found,' Jarred broke in.

They turned from each other to look at him. 'We will discuss this further at the forge,' he said rapidly. 'For the moment, remember that now that Prandine is dead, no-one knows that you have a friend outside the palace. The Shadow Lord will not suspect that a humble blacksmith could be a threat to him.'

'*You* will go now, to find the gems?' whispered Endon.

Jarred shook his head. 'I would not succeed now, any more than you would do, Endon. Our enemy's servants will be watching the gems' hiding places for signs that they are in danger. But in years to come the Shadow Lord will begin to believe that he is safe and the watching will become less. Then, and only then, the quest can begin.'

He held out his uninjured hand to Endon. 'After this day we may not meet again in this life, my friend,' he said in a low voice. 'We will be far apart, and who can tell what will become of us in the dangerous times ahead? But one day the gems will be found and the Belt will be restored. It will be done.'

Endon took the hand in both his own and bowed his head. Then, suddenly, the walls of the chapel trembled as though the palace had been struck by a great wind.

'We must go!' Sharn cried in alarm.

As he helped her climb into the tunnel entrance, Endon turned to Jarred. 'You say we must run, that we must hide, but where can we go?' he asked in a trembling voice.

'With the Shadow Lord will come a time of confusion and darkness,' Jarred answered grimly. 'Many people will be roaming the countryside, neighbour will lose sight of neighbour, and life will not be as it was before. The confusion will aid us.'

'You have thought of a place?' whispered Endon.

'Perhaps,' muttered Jarred. 'It will be dangerous, but if you are willing, the chance is worth taking.'

Endon asked no more, but followed his wife into the tunnel. Jarred climbed after him, pulling the marble tile back into place over his head so that no-one could tell where they had gone.

As the last of the light from the chapel was shut out and blackness enfolded him, he thought of Anna and his heart ached.

The life they had known had been hard, but they had been happy. Now all this was ended. Fear and trouble were coming—long years of waiting while Deltora groaned under the yoke of the Shadow Lord.

And only time could tell what would happen then.

PART II: UNDER THE SHADOW

8 - Lief

Lief ran for home down the dark, winding backstreets of Del, past lighted houses closed tightly for the night. He ran as fast and silently as a cat, his heart hammering in his chest.

He was late. Very late. He had to hurry, but he knew that the smallest sound could betray him.

It was forbidden to be on the streets after sunset. That was one of the Shadow Lord's strictest laws. It had been put into force on the day he took possession of Del, just over sixteen years ago. The penalty for breaking it was death.

Lief slipped into a long, narrow street that ran through the ruined part of the city. It smelt of damp and decay. The stones under his feet were slimy and treacherous.

He had been out after sunset before, but not for so long and never so far from home. He wished with all his heart that he had been more careful. It flashed through his mind that his father and mother would be waiting for him, worried for him.

'You are free for the afternoon, my son,' his father had said, when their midday meal was over. 'Your sixteenth birthday is a special day. Your mother and I want you to be glad and to celebrate with your friends.'

Lief was overjoyed. Never before had he been granted leave in the middle of the working day. Usually he had to study in the afternoons.

He had always felt that this was unfair. He was the only one of his friends who had lessons to do. Why learn to read and write? Why learn figures and history and worry at mind-games? Of what use were these things to a blacksmith?

But his parents had insisted that the lessons go on, and, grumbling, Lief had obeyed. Now he was used to the way things were. But this did not mean that he liked them any the better. A free afternoon was the best birthday gift he could imagine.

'Tonight, there will be another gift. And—things we must discuss together,' his father said, exchanging looks with his mother.

Lief glanced at their grave faces with quick curiosity. 'What things?' he asked.

His mother smiled and shook her head. 'We will talk of them tonight, Lief,' she said, pushing him gently towards the door. 'For now, enjoy your holiday. But stay out of trouble. And keep track of the time, I beg you. Be home well before sunset.'

Lief promised gladly and ran—out of the house, through the hot forge where he helped his father each morning, past Barda, the tattered, half-wit beggar who sat all day at the gate and slept in the forge yard by night. He crossed the road that led to the palace on the hill and waded through the weed-filled fields beyond. Then he ran joyfully on till he reached the market, where he could lose himself in the smells and sounds of the noisy, crowded city.

He found one of his friends, then another, then three more. Happily they roamed their favourite haunts together. They had no money to spend but they found fun anyway—teasing the stall-holders in the markets, running up and down the grimy alley-ways, dodging the Grey Guards, looking for silver coins in the choked and overflowing gutters. Then, in a deserted and overgrown patch of ground not far from the palace walls, they found something better than silver—a twisted old tree covered in small, round red fruits.

'Apples!' Lief knew what the fruits were. He had even tasted an apple, once. It was when he was very young. In those days there were still some large orchards in the city. Apples and other fruits could be bought in the markets, though they were costly. But years ago it had been declared that all fruits of Del were the property of the Shadow Lord, wherever the trees that bore them grew.

This tree had somehow been forgotten, and there were no Guards to be seen.

Lief and his friends picked as many of the apples as they could carry and went down into the drain-tunnels under the city to eat them in secret. The fruits were small and spotted, but they were sweet. It was a feast, enjoyed all the better for knowing that it was stolen from the hated Shadow Lord.

An hour before sunset, Lief's friends left him and hurried home. Lief, however, was unwilling to waste his last hour of freedom. He stayed in the silence and dimness of the drains, exploring and thinking.

He meant to stay only a little while, but then he discovered a small drain-tunnel branching off the main, leading, he was sure, towards the palace on the hill. He crept along this new tunnel as far as he dared then turned back, promising himself that he would follow it further another day. But when, finally, he crawled up to the surface, he found that time had rushed by. Night had fallen.

So now he was in danger.

Lief skidded to a stop as two Grey Guards turned a corner in front of him and began pacing in his direction. They were talking and had not yet heard him, seen him, or caught his scent. But when they did . . .

He held his breath, desperately looking this way and that, seeking a way of escape. High walls rose on either side of him, dripping with slimy water and slippery with moss. He could never climb them unaided. He could not turn and run, either. To do so would mean certain death.

Lief had prowled Del's streets all his life, and often

met with danger. He prided himself on his many lucky escapes in the past. He was fast, agile and daring. But he had sense, too—sense enough to know that he could not run the length of this street without being cut down.

Each Guard carried a sling and a supply of what the people of Del called 'blisters'. The blisters were silver eggs filled with burning poison. They burst on contact with a target and the Guards could hurl them with deadly strength and accuracy, even in darkness. Lief had seen enough blister victims fall, writhing in agony, to know that he did not want to risk the same fate.

Yet if he stayed where he was the Guards would come upon him and he would die in any case. By blister or by dagger, he would die.

Lief flattened himself against the wall, still as a shadow, not daring to move a muscle. The Guards paced on towards him. Closer, closer . . .

If only they would turn around! he thought feverishly. If only something would distract them! Then I would have a chance.

He was not praying for a miracle, because he did not believe in miracles. Few citizens of Del did, these days. So he was astounded when a moment later there was a clatter from the corner behind the Guards. They spun around and began running towards the sound.

Hardly able to believe his luck, Lief turned to run. Then, with a shock, he felt something hit his shoulder. To his amazement he saw that it was a rope—a rope dangling from the top of the wall. Who had thrown it?

There was no time to think or wonder. In seconds, he was climbing for his life. He did not pause for breath until he had reached the top of the wall and swung himself into a great tree on the other side. Panting, he huddled in a fork between two branches and looked around him.

He was alone. The rope had been tied securely around the tree's trunk, but there was no sign of whoever had thrown it over the wall.

The Guards had still not come back into view, but Lief could hear them nearby, arguing as they searched for whatever had made the sound they had heard. He was fairly certain that they would find nothing. He was sure that the person who had thrown the rope had also hurled a stone to distract them. That was what he himself would have done if he had been trying to save a friend.

A friend? Lief bit his lip as he swiftly pulled the rope up after him. As far as he knew, all his friends were safely in their homes. Who could have known that he was in trouble?

He puzzled about it for a moment, then shook his head. This is not important now, he told himself. The important thing is to reach home before anything else happens.

He untied the rope, coiled it and slung it over his shoulder. Ropes such as these were valuable.

He climbed silently to the ground and strained his eyes to see through the darkness. Slowly he recognised the shape nearest to him. It was an old potter's wheel, broken and lying on its side in the grass.

With a chill he realised that he was in the backyard of what had been the city's biggest pottery. A thousand times he had walked past its burned-out shell, its gaping front windows and its door branded with the Shadow Lord's sign.

The brand meant that the Shadow Lord's hand had been laid upon the pottery. Now it was a dead place, never again to be used, or even entered. There were many such buildings, and many such signs, in this part of the city. A group here had tried to resist the Shadow Lord. They had plotted to overthrow him. But he had found out, as he found out all such secrets.

Lief threaded his way through the huge piles of smashed pots, overgrown with weeds. He passed the two great ovens where the pots had been baked, now just ruined heaps of bricks. He nearly tripped on something buried in the grass—a child's wooden horse, crushed under the foot of a Grey Guard long ago.

By the time he reached the front of the building

he was trembling and breathing hard. Not with fear now, but with a sudden, terrible anger.

Why should his people suffer this? Why should he have to creep around in his own city like a criminal, in fear of branding, imprisonment or death?

He moved out onto the deserted road and looked up at the palace on the hill, sick with loathing. For as long as he could remember the palace had been the headquarters of the Shadow Lord. Before that, his friends had told him, the king of Deltora had lived there, in luxury, and the palace was almost hidden by a pale, shimmering mist. But when the Shadow Lord came, the mist completely disappeared. Now the palace could be seen clearly.

Though Lief's parents had made him study the history of Deltora from its earliest days, they had told him little of the time just before he was born. They seemed to fear speaking of it. They said the Shadow Lord had spies everywhere, and it was best to keep silence. But Lief's friends were not afraid, and they had told him a great deal.

They had told him that the last king, like the rulers before him, had cared nothing for the people, and done nothing to serve them. King Endon's only task had been to guard the magic Belt of Deltora. But he had been weak, lazy and careless. He had allowed the Belt to be stolen. He had opened the way to the Shadow Lord.

The king was dead, Lief's friends said. And a good thing, too, Lief thought savagely, as again he hurried for home. The king deserved to die for the suffering he had brought to his people.

He reached the fields and began to run, crouching low, hiding himself in the long grass. A few minutes more, and he would be safe. Already he could see the lights of home winking dimly in the distance.

He knew he would be in trouble for being so late and that there would be questions asked about the rope he carried. With luck, though, his mother and father would be so relieved to see him that they would forgive him quickly.

They cannot send me to bed without food, at least, Lief thought with satisfaction, scuttling across the road and plunging on towards the forge. They said they wanted to talk to me about something tonight.

Briefly he wondered what that something was, and smiled at the memory of how serious his parents had looked when they had spoken of it.

He loved them both very much, but no two people could be more ordinary, timid and quiet than Jarred and Anna of the forge. Jarred had limped badly ever since he was injured by a falling tree when Lief was ten. But even before that, he and Anna had kept very much to themselves. They seemed content to listen to the tales of wandering travellers who stopped at the forge, rather than seeing life for themselves.

Lief had not been born until after the time of darkness and terror that had marked the coming of the Shadow Lord. But he knew that many in the city had fought and died and many others had fled in terror.

Jarred and Anna had done neither of these things. While all around them confusion and panic reigned, they stayed in their cottage, obeying every order given to them, doing nothing to attract the anger of the enemy. And when the panic was ended and dull misery had taken its place in the city, they re-opened the forge gates and began work again, struggling only to survive in their new, ruined world.

It was something that Lief himself could never have done. He could not understand it. He was convinced that all his parents had ever wanted in their lives was to stay out of trouble, whatever the cost. He was certain, absolutely certain, that nothing they had to say could surprise him.

So it was only with relief that he ran through the forge gates, dodged the beggar Barda, who was making his slow way to his shelter in the corner of the yard, and rushed through the cottage door. Excuses were ready on his tongue and thoughts of dinner were filling his head.

Little did he know that before another hour had passed everything was going to change for him.

Little did he know that he was about to receive the shock of his life.

9 - The Secret

Stunned by what he had just heard, Lief stared at his father. It was as if he was seeing him with new eyes. '*You* once lived in the palace? *You* were the king's friend? You—I cannot believe this! I will *not* believe it!'

His father smiled grimly. 'You must believe it, my son.' His fists clenched. 'Why else do you think we have lived so quietly all these years, tamely obeying every order given to us, never rebelling? Many, many times I have been tempted to do otherwise. But I knew that we had to avoid drawing the enemy's attention to us.'

'But—but why have you never told me before?' Lief stammered.

'We thought it best to keep silent until now, Lief.' It was his mother who had spoken. She stood by the fire looking at him gravely.

'It was so important, you see, that no word reached

the ears of the Shadow Lord,' she went on. 'And until you were ten your father believed that he himself would be the one who would go to seek the gems of Deltora, when the time came. But then—'

She broke off, glancing at her husband sitting in his armchair, his injured leg stuck stiffly out in front of him.

He smiled grimly. 'Then the tree fell, and I had to accept that this could not be,' he finished for her. 'I can still work in the forge—enough to earn our bread—but I cannot travel. And so, Lief, the task is left to you. If you are willing.'

Lief's head was spinning. So much that he had believed had been overturned in one short hour.

'The king was not killed after all,' he mumbled, trying to take it in. 'He escaped, with the queen. But why did the Shadow Lord not find them?'

'When we reached the forge the king and queen made themselves look like ordinary working people,' his father said. 'In haste we discussed the plan for escape while outside the wind howled and the darkness of the Shadow Lord deepened over the land. And then we parted.'

His face was furrowed with grief and memory. 'We knew that we might never meet again. Endon had realised by then that by his foolishness and blindness the people's last trust in him had been destroyed. The Belt would never again shine for him. All our hopes rested with his unborn child.'

'But—how do you know that the child was born safely and is still alive, Father?' Lief blurted out.

His father heaved himself to his feet. He took off the old brown belt that he always wore at his work. It was strong and heavy, made of two lengths of leather stitched together. He cut the stitching at one end with his knife and pulled out what was hidden inside.

Lief caught his breath. Sliding from the leather tube was a fine steel chain linking seven steel medallions. Even plain and without ornament, it was still the most beautiful thing he had ever seen.

He longed to touch it. Eagerly he held out his hands.

'I mended it, making it ready to receive the gems once more, before I hid it away,' his father said, handing it to him. 'But so closely is it bound to the blood of Adin that it would have crumbled into pieces if the heir was no more. As you see, it is still whole. So we can be sure that the heir lives.'

In wonder, Lief gazed at the marvellous thing in his hands—the dream Belt made by the great Adin himself. How many times had he read of it in *The Belt of Deltora*, the small, pale blue book his father had given him to study? He could hardly believe that he was actually holding it.

'If you agree to go on the quest, my son, you must put the Belt on and never let it out of your sight until it is complete,' he heard his mother say. 'Are you willing? Think carefully before you answer.'

But Lief had already made his decision. He looked

up at his waiting parents, his eyes sparkling.

'I am willing,' he said firmly. Without hesitation he clasped the Belt around his waist, under his shirt. It felt cool against his skin. 'Where must I go, to find the gems?' he asked.

His father, suddenly drawn and pale, sat down again, and stared at the fire. 'Preparing for this moment we have listened to many travellers' tales,' he said at last. 'I will tell you what we know. Prandine said that the gems were scattered, hidden in places no-one would dare to find them.'

'That means, I suppose, that they lie in places people would be afraid to go,' Lief said.

'So I fear.' His father picked up a parchment from the table beside his chair and began slowly to unfold it. 'Seven Ak-Baba were flying together around the palace tower on the day the gems were taken,' he went on. 'They separated and flew off in different directions. We believe that each was carrying one of the gems, and each was going to one particular place to hide it. See here. I have drawn a map.'

His heart beating like a drum in his chest, Lief leaned over to look as his father pointed out one name after the other.

'The Lake of Tears,' Lief read. 'City of the Rats. The Shifting Sands. Dread Mountain. The Maze of the Beast. The Valley of the Lost, The Forests of Silence . . .' His voice faltered. The very names filled him with fear, particularly the last.

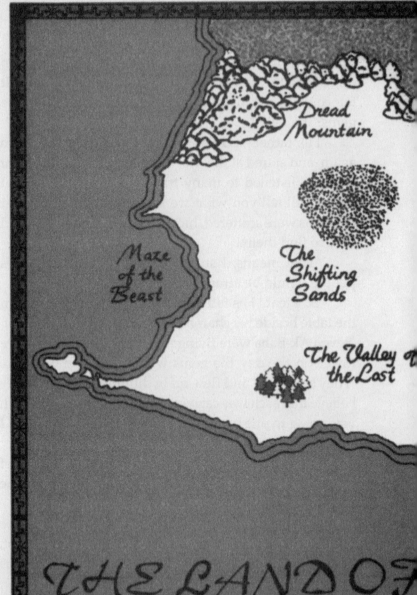

Dread
Mountain

Maze
of the
Beast

The
Shifting
Sands

The Valley of
the Lost

THE LAND OF

The Shadowlands
The Lake of Tears
City of the Rats
The Forests of Silence
Del
N
W
E
S
DELTORA

The terrible tales he had heard of the Forests not far to the east of Del flooded Lief's mind, and for a moment the map blurred before his eyes.

'Over the years, different travellers have told of seeing a lone Ak-Baba hovering above one or another of these seven places on the day the Shadow Lord came,' his father was saying. 'They are where you must search for the gems, we are sure of it. Little is known of them, but all of them have evil reputations. The task will be long and perilous, Lief. Are you still willing?'

Lief's mouth felt dry. He swallowed, and nodded.

'He is so young!' his mother burst out. She bent her head and hid it in her hands. 'Oh, I cannot bear it!'

Lief spun around to her and threw his arm around her neck. 'I *want* to go, Mother!' he exclaimed. 'Do not weep for me.'

'You do not know what you are promising!' she cried.

'Perhaps I do not,' Lief admitted. 'But I know that I would do anything—anything in my power—to rid our land of the Shadow Lord.'

He turned from her to look back at his father. 'Where is the heir?' he demanded excitedly. 'That, at least, you know for certain, Father, for you suggested the hiding place.'

'Perhaps I did,' his father said quietly. 'But I must not endanger our cause by telling you of it. The heir is powerless without the Belt, and must remain in deepest hiding until it is complete. You are young and impatient,

Lief, and the road ahead of you is hard. You might give way to temptation and seek out the heir before your quest is done. I cannot risk that.'

Lief opened his mouth to argue, but his father held up his hand, shaking his head. 'When the gems are all in place the Belt will lead you to the heir, my son,' he said firmly. 'You must wait until then.'

He half-smiled as Lief sighed with frustration. Then he bent down and drew something from under his chair.

'Perhaps this will cheer you,' he said. 'It is my birthday gift to you.'

Lief stared at the slender, shining sword in his father's hand. Never had he expected to own such a blade.

'I made it on our own forge,' his father said, giving the sword to him. 'It is the finest work I have ever done. Care for it well, and it will care for you.'

As Lief nodded, spluttering his thanks, he became aware that his mother, too, was holding out a gift. It was a finely-woven cloak—soft, light and warm. Its colour seemed to change as it moved so that it was hard to tell if it was brown, green or grey. Somewhere between all three, Lief decided at last. Like river-water in autumn.

'This, too, will care for you, wherever you may go,' his mother whispered, pressing the cloak into his hands and kissing him. 'The fabric is—special. I used every art I knew in its making, and wove much love and many memories into it, as well as strength and warmth.'

Her husband stood up and put his arm around her. She leaned against him lovingly, but tears shone in her eyes.

Lief looked at them both. 'You never doubted that I would agree to go on this quest,' he said quietly.

'We knew you too well to doubt it,' his mother answered, trying to smile. 'I was sure, as well, that you would want to start at once. Food and water for the first few days of your journey are already packed and waiting. You can leave within the hour, if you wish.'

'Tonight?' gasped Lief. His stomach turned over. He had not thought it would be so soon. And yet almost immediately he realised that his mother was right. Now that the decision had been made, he wanted nothing more than to begin.

'There is one thing more,' his father said, limping to the door. 'You will not be alone on your quest. You will have a companion.'

Lief's jaw dropped. Were the surprises of this night never to end?

'Who—?' he began.

'A good friend. The one man we know we can trust,' his father answered gruffly. He swung the door open.

And, to Lief's horror, into the room shuffled Barda, the beggar.

10 - Decisions

S o, Lief,' Barda mumbled. 'Are you not pleased with your companion?'

Lief could only stand gaping at him.

'Do not tease him, Barda.' Smiling, Lief's mother moved to her son's side and gently touched his shoulder. 'How could Lief know you are other than you appear to be? Explain yourself!'

Barda pulled off the ragged cloak he wore, letting it fall to the floor at his feet. Underneath the cloak his garments were rough, but clean. He straightened his shoulders, pushed back his tousled hair from his face, tightened his jaw and lifted his head. Suddenly he looked completely different—tall, strong and many years younger.

'I also lived in the palace, when your father and King Endon were young, Lief,' he said, in quite a different voice. 'I was the grown son of their nursemaid, Min, but they did not know me, or I them. While they were at their lessons I was already in training as a palace guard.'

'But—but all my life you have lived outside the forge,' Lief stammered.

Barda's face darkened. 'I left the palace on the night my mother was killed. I knew that I would suffer the same fate, if I stayed. My guard's uniform helped me to trick my way through the gates, and I came here.'

Lief swallowed. 'Why here?'

'Fate guided me, I believe, as it had guided Jarred before me,' Barda answered quietly. 'It was deepest night. The cottage was in darkness. I hid myself in the forge, and slept. When at last I stirred, many hours later, it was day, though it did not seem so. A terrible wind was howling. Only half-awake, I stumbled outside and saw four strangers by the gate. I know now that they were Jarred and Anna hurrying the king and queen away, but then I knew nothing.'

He glanced at Lief's father. 'Jarred was rather startled to see a palace guard lurching toward him,' he added dryly. 'He greeted me with a blow that put me back to sleep for quite some time.'

Lief shook his head, hardly able to believe that his gentle father would strike anyone.

'When I woke again I found that Jarred and Anna no longer feared me,' Barda went on. 'While I was unconscious I had rambled aloud of my grief and fear, so they knew who I was and well understood the danger that threatened me. They knew I was a friend.'

'So we did,' murmured Lief's mother. She turned to Lief. 'We told Barda who our visitors had been. We asked for his help in seeking the lost gems of Deltora when the time came.'

Barda frowned grimly. 'I agreed willingly. I had already decided that I would do anything to overthrow the Shadow Lord, and avenge my mother's death.'

'It—it is incredible!' Lief spluttered. 'All this time you . . .'

Barda shrugged. 'All this time I have been safe, hidden in my beggar's disguise. Jarred and Anna have given me food and shelter, and helped me to play my part without too much suffering. In return, I have watched over you since you were ten years old—'

'Watched over me?' Lief gasped.

'Oh, yes,' drawled Barda. 'After your father was injured I said that I would go alone on the quest for the gems, when the time came. But Jarred and Anna—felt differently. They believed that you should be given the chance to fulfil your father's pledge.'

He glanced at Lief's parents as he spoke. They remained expressionless, but it was clear to Lief that there had been many arguments on this subject in the past. Barda would plainly have preferred to travel alone.

He thinks that I will be a burden to him, Lief thought angrily. But before he could say anything, Barda went on.

'I agreed to your company, on the condition that

you be allowed to sharpen your wits and learn of life by roaming free in the city. I believed that this was as important as your book learning and your sword-play in fitting you for the time ahead. But of course you had to be protected from real harm, without your knowledge.'

His lips twitched into a smile. 'It has not been easy, young Lief, keeping you out of trouble. And this reminds me. You have my rope, I believe?' He held out his hand.

Not daring to look at his parents, Lief passed over the coil of rope he had thrown down in a corner. His face had grown hot as he remembered how he had prided himself on his many lucky escapes over the years, and boasted of them to his friends. So they had not been a matter of luck, or skill. Barda had been his bodyguard all along.

He looked down at the floor, his stomach churning with furious shame. What a fool he must think me! he raged silently. This—this *child* he had to mind like a nurse! How he must have laughed at me!

He became aware that Barda was speaking again, and forced himself to look up.

'My beggar's rags have been useful in other ways,' the man was saying, calmly fastening the rope to his belt. 'Grey Guards talk freely to each other in front of me. Why should they care what a half-wit beggar hears?'

'It is because of news Barda has gathered in the past year, Lief, that we know it is time to make our move,' Lief's father added, eyeing his son's grim face anxiously. 'Hungry for further conquest, the Shadow

Lord has at last turned his eyes away from us, to lands across the sea. Warships are being launched from our coast.'

'There are still many Grey Guards in the city, but few now patrol the countryside, it seems,' Barda added. 'They have left it to the bands of robbers, and to the other horrors that now run wild there. There have always been terrors and evil beings in Deltora, but once they were balanced by the good. With the coming of the Shadow Lord, the balance ended. Evil has become much more powerful.'

A chill ran through Lief, quenching his anger. But Barda's eyes were upon him, and he would rather have died than show his fear. He snatched up the map. 'Have you decided on our route?' he asked abruptly.

His father seemed about to speak, but Barda answered first, pointing to a spot on the map with a blunt finger. 'I believe we should move east, directly to the Forests of Silence.'

Three gasps of shock sounded in the small room.

Lief's father cleared his throat. 'We had decided that the Forests should be your final ordeal, not your first, Barda,' he said huskily.

Barda shrugged. 'I heard something today that changed my mind. The Grey Guards have always feared the Forests, as we have. But now, it seems, no Guard will even approach them, because of the losses they have suffered. The roads around them are completely clear— of Guards, at least.'

Stiff with shock, Lief stared at the map with glazed eyes. To face the Forests of Silence, that place of childhood nightmare, at some time in the future was one thing. To face it so soon, in a matter of days, was another.

'What think you, Lief?' he heard Barda say.

His voice was casual, but Lief was sure that the question was a test. He wet his lips and looked up from the map, meeting the tall man's gaze steadily. 'Your plan seems to me a good one, Barda,' he said. 'With no Guards to trouble us, we will make good time. And if we can find one gem quickly, it will give us good heart to go on.'

Barda's eyes flickered. I was right, thought Lief. He thought I would refuse to go with him. He thought to be rid of me. Well, he was wrong.

'So, Jarred?' Barda asked gruffly.

The blacksmith bowed his head. 'It seems fate has taken a hand to alter my plans,' he murmured. 'I must bow to it. Do as you will. Our thoughts and hopes go with you.'

11 - Beware!

Many hours later, feeling as though he was living in a dream, Lief was marching east along the road leading away from Del. Barda strode beside him, silent, upright and strong—a completely different person from the shambling, mumbling wreck who had haunted the gates of the forge for as long as Lief could remember.

They had left Del unnoticed by creeping through a hole in the wall that Lief had not known existed, so cleverly was it disguised. Now the city, his parents and everything he knew were far behind him, and with every step he was moving towards a place whose very name made him sweat with fear.

The Forests of Silence strike a special terror in my heart, for they are near, and I have heard tales of them all my life, he told himself. But it is certain that the other places on the map are just as deadly in their own way.

This idea did not comfort him in the least.

For the first hour after leaving the city he had walked with his hand on his sword, his heart thumping. But they met no-one, and for a long time now he had been concentrating only on moving quickly, keeping up with Barda's long strides. He was determined not to be the one to call for rest. Determined, too, not to be the first to speak, though his head was teeming with questions.

They came to a place where a small road branched off the main one to the right, crossing a little wooden bridge and then winding away into the darkness. Barda stopped.

'I believe that this is the path to Wenn Del—and the shortest way to the Forests,' he said. 'The turning fits the description I was given. But there should be a signpost, and there is none.'

Tall trees rose around them, but no leaves rustled. The silence was heavy and complete. It was as if the land was holding its breath, waiting for them to decide what to do.

The clouds parted for a moment, and the moon's ghostly light beamed down on them. Looking around, Lief saw a tiny glimmer of white on the ground by the side of the road. He moved to it quickly, knelt down, then beckoned to Barda.

'It is here,' he called excitedly, scrabbling among the dead leaves. 'Someone has pushed it over, to keep the way secret.'

The signpost lay flat on the ground, almost covered

by leaves and small plants. Lief brushed away the last of the leaves, then sat back on his heels with a gasp as he saw what was underneath.

'Someone has tried to warn other travellers of danger along this path. No doubt the sign was not pushed over to hide the way, but to hide the warning,' Barda muttered.

Lief stood up slowly, glancing behind him. Suddenly the silence seemed thick and heavy, pressing in on him.

He became aware that his companion was watching him, frowning. 'This path will save us a day and a half, if we take it,' Barda said. 'But perhaps I should not lead you into certain peril when we have just begun.'

All at once, Lief was very angry. With Barda for seeing his fear, with himself for showing that fear and, most of all, with the unknown enemy who had so craftily hidden the warning sign.

'You do not have to guard my safety any longer, Barda,' he said loudly, kicking at the dead leaves. 'A short cut is too precious to waste. We are prepared for trouble, now. We will watch for danger as we go.'

'Very well,' said Barda, turning away. 'As you wish.' His voice was as calm and level as always. Lief could not tell if he was pleased or sorry.

They turned to the right, crossed the little bridge, and went on. The road twisted, narrowed, and became darker. Tall, thick bushes lined it on both sides. Their leaves were large, smooth and stiff, with strange, pale veins showing almost white against the dark green.

They had not gone far before the back of Lief's neck began to prickle. He turned his head slightly, and, from the corner of his eye, caught a glimpse of something gleaming through the leaves. It was a pair of red eyes, glinting in the moonlight. Controlling his urge to shout, he touched Barda's arm.

'I see them,' Barda muttered. 'Draw your sword, but keep walking. Look to the front. Be ready.'

Lief did as he was told, his whole body tingling with alarm. He saw another pair of eyes, and another. And soon it seemed that the whole path was lined with burning points of light. But still there was no sound.

He gritted his teeth. The hand that held the sword was slippery with sweat. 'What are they? What are they waiting for?' he hissed to Barda.

As he spoke something skittered across the road behind him. He swung around just in time to see a creature disappearing into the bushes—a bent, pale, scuttling thing that seemed all legs and arms. His skin crawled.

'Look ahead!' hissed Barda, furiously dragging on

his arm to make him move again. 'Didn't I tell you—'

And then the humming began.

The sound was soft, at first. It came from all around them, filling the air—a high, whining hum, as if a great swarm of flying insects had suddenly invaded the road.

But no insects were to be seen. Only the dark green of the leaves. And the eyes, watching. And the sound, which grew louder and louder with every step they took, so that soon their heads were filled with it, and their ears began to ache and ring.

And still the sound rose—high, piercing, unbearable. Desperate to shut it out they clapped their hands to their ears and bent their heads against it, walking fast, faster—breaking into a run. Their feet thudded on the endless path, their breath came hard and panting, their hearts beat like thunder. But they were aware of nothing—nothing but the pain of the sound that rose and rose, piercing their brains, driving out every thought.

They ran, weaving and stumbling, desperate to escape it. But there was no escape. They cried out for help But they could not even hear their own voices. Finally they fell, exhausted, to lie writhing, helpless in the dust.

The sound rose to an agonising wail of triumph. The leaves thrashed and rustled. A host of pale, lanky creatures with hot red eyes scuttled towards them.

And, in moments, they were covered.

✳

Lief woke slowly, with no idea of where he was, or how much time had passed. There was a dull ringing in his ears. His throat was raw. Every muscle in his body was aching.

I am alive, he thought, with dull surprise. How is it that I am alive?

He struggled to think, though his brain seemed clouded by a thick fog.

The last he remembered was running with Barda along the Wenn Del path, his head almost bursting with sound. After that there was only blankness.

Or was there? He seemed to remember a dream. A dream of needle-sharp, stinging pains all over his body. A dream of being poked and prodded by thin, hard fingers. A dream of being carried, jolting, on bony shoulders. A dream of shrill tittering and muttering, while night turned into day and day to night again.

A terrible dream. But . . . had it been a dream? Or had it been real? Had it all been real?

He was lying on his back. Light slanted through branches high above him. It is day now, then, Lief thought drowsily. Late afternoon, by the look of it. But which afternoon? How long have I been unconscious? And where am I?

He heard a groan nearby. He tried to turn his head. And it was only then that he realised that he could not move.

Panic seized him. He tried to lift his hands, move his feet. But he could not even twitch a finger.

How could they have bound me so completely? he thought stupidly.

And slowly, horribly the answer came to him. He was not tied up at all. His body was simply refusing to move at his will.

'What—has happened?' he cried aloud, in terror.

'They stung us—as wasps sting caterpillars, as spiders sting flies.' Barda's voice was thick and slow, but Lief recognised it. He realised that it was Barda who had groaned. Barda was lying near to him. Barda was as helpless as he was.

'The creatures have paralysed us so that we still live, but cannot move,' Barda's voice went on. 'They will be back, and then they will feast.'

Again he groaned. 'We were fools to ignore the warning sign. I am to blame. I could not imagine a weapon we could not fight. But that sound! No-one could stand against it. I cannot understand why the Guards in Del did not speak of it.'

'Perhaps they did not know. Perhaps no-one who has ever heard the sound has lived to tell of it,' said Lief.

'Lief—I have led you to your death!'

Lief licked his dry lips. 'It is not your fault. We took the road together. And we are not dead yet! Barda—where are we?'

The answer came even more slowly than before, and when it came it filled Lief's heart with dread. 'They carried us a long way,' Barda said weakly. 'I think—I think we are in the Forests of Silence.'

Lief closed his eyes, trying to fight the wave of

despair that was sweeping over him. And then a thought came to him.

'Why?' he asked. 'Why bring us here, to a place so far from their home?'

'Because,' called a new voice, 'you are too great a prize for the Wenn alone. They have brought you as an offering for their god. The Wennbar likes fresh meat. It will come when the sun goes down.'

There was a rustle from the tree above. And, as lightly as a butterfly, a wild-haired girl landed on the ground right beside Lief's head.

12 - The Wennbar

Astounded, Lief blinked up at the girl. She was about his own age, elfin-faced, with black hair, slanting black brows and green eyes. She was dressed in ragged grey clothes that seemed strangely familiar. She was bending over him, unfastening the ties of his cloak.

'Thank heavens you have come!' he whispered.

'This will be useful, Filli,' the girl said.

With a shock, Lief realised that she was not speaking to him, but to a small, furry, wide-eyed creature that was clinging to her shoulder.

'How lucky that we came this way today,' she went on. 'If we had left it until tomorrow the cloth would have been quite spoiled.'

With a single push of her slim, sun-browned arm, she rolled Lief onto his side so that she could pull the cloak from beneath him. Then she let him roll back and stood up, the cloak draped carelessly over her arm.

A harsh cry came from overhead. Lief raised his eyes and saw a black bird, a raven, perched in the tree from which the girl had leapt. Its head on one side, it was watching them carefully with one sharp yellow eye.

The girl grinned and held up the cloak. 'See what I have found, Kree!' she called. 'A fine new blanket for the nest. But we are coming back now. Do not fear.'

She turned to go.

'No!' shouted Lief in panic. 'Do not leave us!'

'You cannot leave us here to die!' Barda roared at the same moment. But already the girl had disappeared from sight, taking the cloak with her. And suddenly, in the midst of his despair, Lief thought of his mother's hands, patiently weaving the cloth by candlelight.

'Bring back my cloak!' he bellowed.

Even as he shouted, he knew how foolish it was. He was going to die, horribly, very soon. What did it matter if the cloak was gone?

But somehow it *did* matter. 'You have no right to take it!' he shouted furiously to the empty air. 'My mother made it for me. My mother!'

There was a moment's silence. Then, to Lief's astonishment, the girl was back, staring down at him suspiciously through the tangled mass of her hair.

'How could your mother have made this cloak?' she demanded. 'Grey Guards do not know their mothers. They are raised in groups of ten, in houses with—'

'I am not a Grey Guard!' shouted Lief. 'My friend

and I are—travellers, from Del. Can you not see by our garments?'

The girl laughed scornfully. 'Your disguise does not fool me. Only Grey Guards take the Wenn Del path, for it leads nowhere but to the Forests.'

She raised her hand to caress the little animal clinging to her shoulder, and her voice hardened. 'Many of your fellows have been here before you, seeking living things to take or destroy. They have learned painfully of their mistake.'

'We are not Guards,' Barda called out. 'My name is Barda. My companion is Lief. We came to the Forests for good reason.'

'What reason?' the girl demanded disbelievingly.

'We—we cannot tell you,' said Lief.

She turned away, shrugging. With a surge of panic Lief shouted after her. 'What is your name? Where is your family? Can you bring them here?'

The girl paused and turned back to look at him again. She seemed puzzled, as though no-one had ever asked her such things before. 'My name is Jasmine,' she said, at last. 'Kree and Filli are my family. Grey Guards took my mother and father long ago.'

Lief's heart sank. So there was no-one to help her carry them to safety. But still . . . she was strong. Perhaps even now there was some way . . .

'The Grey Guards are our deadly enemies, as they are yours,' he said, as calmly and forcefully as he could. 'Our quest to the forest is part of a plan to defeat them—

to rid Deltora of the Shadow Lord. Help us, we beg you!'

He held his breath as the girl hesitated, fingering the cloak she still held over her arm. Then, above their heads, the black bird screeched again. Jasmine glanced up at it, threw the cloak down onto Lief's chest and darted away without another word.

'Come back!' cried Lief, with all his strength. 'Jasmine!' But there was no reply, and when he looked up to the tree again, even the bird had gone.

Lief heard Barda moan once, in helpless anger. Then there was utter silence. No bird sang. No small creature rustled in the grass. It was the silence of waiting. The silence of despair. The silence of death.

The sun sank lower in the sky. Long, dark shadows striped the place where they lay. Soon, very soon, it would be dark. And then, thought Lief, then the Wennbar will come.

The cloak felt warm on his chest. He could not lift a hand to touch it, but still it gave him comfort. He was glad that it was with him. He closed his eyes . . .

✳

Something gripped his shoulder. He cried out in terror and opened his eyes to see Jasmine's face close to his.

'Open your mouth!' the girl ordered. 'Make haste!' She pushed a tiny bottle towards his lips.

Confused, Lief did as he was told. He felt two cold drops fall on his tongue. A horrible taste filled his mouth.

'What—?' he spluttered.

But Jasmine had already turned away from him.

'Open your mouth!' he heard her hissing to Barda.

A moment later Barda made a choking, disgusted sound. Lief realised that he, too, had been given some of the vile-tasting liquid.

'Poison!' Barda rasped. 'You—'

Lief's heart gave a great thud. Then, suddenly, his body grew hot and began to prickle all over. With every instant the feeling grew stronger and more frightening. The heat became burning. The prickles became needle-sharp jabs of pain. It was as though he was caught in a flaming thorn bush.

The warning screech of the bird sounded far above them. The sky was red through the leaves of the tree. Barda was crying out. But now Lief could hear nothing, see nothing, feel nothing but his own pain and fear. He began to writhe and thrash on the ground.

Then, dimly, he realised that Jasmine was bending over him. She was pulling at his arms, kicking at him with hard, bare feet. 'Get up!' she was urging. 'Listen to me! Do you not see what you are doing? You are moving! You can move!

You can move! Gasping, hardly able to believe it, Lief fought back the pain and struggled to his hands and knees. Blindly he felt for his cloak. He was not going to leave it now.

'The tree!' Jasmine shouted. 'Crawl to the tree and climb! The Wennbar is almost upon us!' She had already turned to Barda. He was rolling on his bed of ferns, groaning in agony.

Lief hauled himself towards them, dragging his cloak behind him, but the girl waved him back. 'Go!' she cried furiously. 'I will see to him! Go! Climb!'

Lief knew she was right. He could not help her, or Barda. It was as much as he could do to help himself. He began to crawl towards the trunk of the great tree. His legs and arms were trembling. His whole body shuddered, swept by waves of heat.

He reached the tree and pulled himself upright. There was a low branch near his hand. He grasped it, panting, and with the other hand pulled his cloak around him.

Only a day or two ago he had climbed a rope to the top of a high wall without a thought. Now he doubted that he could even haul himself onto this branch.

The clearing dimmed. The sun had slipped below the horizon.

High above Lief there was a clatter of wings as the black bird left its perch. Calling harshly, urgently, it soared down to where Jasmine staggered towards the tree with Barda leaning on her shoulder.

'I know, Kree!' Jasmine gasped, as the bird flapped anxiously around her head. 'I can smell it.'

As she said the words, Lief smelt something, too. A faint, sickening odour of decay was stealing through the clearing.

His stomach turned over. He tied the strings of the cloak, grasped the branch with both hands and managed to pull himself up. He clung to the rough bark, panting and shaking, afraid that even now he might fall.

Jasmine and Barda had reached the tree now, the bird still swooping above them. 'Higher!' Jasmine shouted to Lief. 'As high as you can. It cannot climb, but it will try to claw us down.'

Lief gritted his teeth, lifted his arms and hauled himself to a higher branch. He heard Barda grunting with effort as he struggled to climb after him. The evil smell was stronger, now. And there was a sound—a heavy, stealthy sliding, the snapping of twigs, the rustling of leaves and the cracking of branches as something moved towards the clearing.

'Make haste!' Jasmine had leapt up beside Lief. The tiny creature she called Filli was chattering on her shoulder, its eyes wide with fear.

'Barda—' Lief managed to say.

'He knows what he must do. You can help him only by moving out of his way!' the girl snapped. 'Climb, you fool! Do you not understand! The sun has set. The Wennbar is—'

Filli screamed, the black bird screeched. The bushes on the other side of the clearing thrashed and bent. The air thickened with a smell so vile that Lief choked and gagged. Then a huge, hideous creature, like nothing he had ever seen, crawled into view.

Four stubby legs bent under the weight of a swollen body that was as round, blotched and bloated as some gigantic rotten fruit. Vast, flat feet crushed the twigs beneath them to powder. Folds of wrinkled, green-grey flesh hung from the neck. The head was nothing but two tiny eyes set above long, wicked jaws. The jaws gaped open, showing rows of dripping black teeth and releasing gusts of foul air with every breath.

Choking back a cry of disgust and terror, Lief scrambled higher into the tree, forcing his trembling legs and arms to obey his will. One branch. Then another. And another.

A terrible growl sounded in the clearing. He looked down. Barda and Jasmine were just below him, and they, too, were looking down. The Wennbar had reached the fern bed. It was snapping its jaws together, jerking its head from side to side, growling with anger at finding its prize gone.

We are safe! thought Lief, his heart pounding. Safe! It cannot reach us up here. He closed his eyes, almost dizzy with relief.

'Lief!' shrieked Jasmine.

And Lief opened his eyes just in time to see the Wennbar rear up, its front legs clawing at the air, its pale grey belly gleaming through the dimness. The creature roared, and the folds of skin hanging from its neck disappeared as the neck swelled and grew, raising its head higher, higher . . .

And then it was leaping forward, hurling itself at the tree, its jaws snapping, its tiny eyes burning with rage and hunger.

13 - The Nest

Terror drove Lief upwards. Afterwards, he could not remember climbing for his life while the Wennbar's huge body crashed against the trunk of the tree and its cruel jaws snapped at his heels. He had not had time to draw his sword. He had had no time for anything, but escape.

When he came to himself he was clinging to a high branch, with Jasmine and Barda beside him. The Wennbar's foul breath filled the air. Its roars filled their ears.

They were at last too high for it to reach them, even with its neck fully extended. But it was not giving up. It was dashing itself against the tree, raking the bark with its claws, trying to make them fall.

It was still not completely dark, but it was growing very cold. Lief's cloak kept his body warm but his hands, clinging to the tree, were numb. Beside him, Barda was

91

shivering violently, and his teeth were chattering.

If this goes on, he will fall, Lief thought. He drew as near as he could to Barda and Jasmine. With cold, clumsy fingers he gathered up his cloak and threw it around them so that they could share its warmth.

For a moment they huddled together. And then, Lief realised that something had changed.

The beast had stopped beating itself against the tree. The roars had given way to a low, rumbling growl. Lief felt a movement and realised that Jasmine was peeping through the folds of the cloak to see what was happening.

'It is moving away,' she breathed in wonder. 'It is as though it cannot see us any longer, and thinks we have somehow escaped. But why?'

'The cloak,' whispered Barda feebly. 'The cloak— must be hiding us.'

Lief's heart leapt as he remembered what his mother had said when she gave him the cloak. *This, too, will protect you wherever you go . . . The fabric is—special.*

Just how special?

He heard Jasmine draw a sharp breath. 'What is it?' he hissed.

'The Wenn are coming,' she said. 'I see their eyes. They have heard the roaring cease. They think that the Wennbar has finished with you. They have come for the scraps that remain.'

Lief shuddered. Carefully he moved the cloak aside and peered down to the clearing.

Red eyes were glowing in the bushes, near to where the Wennbar prowled. The creature lifted its head, glared and gave a loud, sharp barking call. It sounded like an order of some kind.

The bushes rustled. The Wennbar called again, even more loudly. And finally two pale, bent shapes crept, quivering, into the clearing to kneel before it.

The Wennbar grunted. Carelessly it seized the kneeling shapes, tossed them into the air, caught them in its hideous jaws and swallowed them whole.

Sickened, Lief turned away from the horrible sight.

Jasmine pushed away the cloak and stood up. 'We are safe, now,' she said. 'See? The Wenn have run away, and the creature is going back to its cave.'

Lief and Barda exchanged glances. 'The cave must be the hiding place,' Barda said in a low voice. 'Tomorrow night, when the creature comes out to feed, we will search it.'

'There is nothing in the Wennbar's cave but bones and stink,' Jasmine snorted. 'What is it you are looking for?'

'We cannot tell you,' said Barda, stiffly hauling himself to his feet. 'But we know that it has been hidden in the most secret place in the Forests of Silence, and that it has a terrible Guardian. Where else could that be, but here?'

To their surprise, Jasmine burst out laughing. 'How little you know!' she cried. 'Why, this is only a tiny corner at the very edge of this one Forest. There are three

Forests in all, and each has a hundred places more dangerous and more secret than this!'

Lief and Barda glanced at one another again as her laughter rang out in the clearing. And then, suddenly, the sound stopped. When they turned to look at her again, she was frowning.

'What is it?' asked Lief.

'It is just...' Jasmine broke off and shook her head. 'We will not speak of it now. I will take you to my nest. There we will be safe. There we can talk.'

✳

They travelled as fast as Lief and Barda were able. As the forest thickened they kept to the treetops almost all the way, climbing from one branch to another, using vines to help them. Above were patches of star-studded sky. Below there was silent darkness. Kree flew ahead of them, stopping to wait when they fell behind. Filli clung to Jasmine's shoulder, his eyes wide and bright.

With every moment, Lief felt his strength returning. But still he was glad when they at last reached Jasmine's home. It was indeed a sort of nest—a big saucer of woven branches and twigs perched high in a huge, twisted tree that grew by itself in a mossy clearing. The moon shone down through the leaves above, flooding the nest with soft, white light.

Jasmine did not speak at once. She made Lief and Barda sit while she brought out berries, fruits, nuts and the hard shell of some sort of melon filled to the brim with sweet, cool water.

Lief rested, looking around in wonder. Jasmine had few possessions. Some of them—like a broken-toothed comb, a tattered sleeping blanket, an old shawl, two tiny bottles and a small, carved wooden doll—were sad reminders of the parents she had lost. Others—a belt, two daggers, several flints to make fire, and many gold and silver coins—had come from the bodies of Grey Guards who had been sacrificed to the Wennbar.

Jasmine was carefully dividing the food and drink into five equal parts, setting out Filli and Kree's places as if they were indeed part of her family. Watching her, Lief realised with a shock that her tattered grey clothes had also come from Grey Guards. She had cut and tied the cloth to fit her.

It made him squirm to think of her robbing helpless victims and leaving them to die. He tried to remember that Guards had taken Jasmine's parents—killed them, probably, or at least enslaved them—and left her alone in this wild forest. But still, her ruthlessness chilled him.

'Eat!'

Jasmine's voice broke into his thoughts. He looked up as she sat down beside him. 'Food will help you to recover,' she said. 'And this food is good.' She helped herself to a strange, pink-coloured fruit and bit into it greedily, the juice running down her chin.

I am a fool to judge her, Lief thought. She lives as best she can. And it is thanks to her that we are alive. She put herself in grave danger for us, when she could have turned her back. Now she has brought us to her home, and shares her food and drink with us.

He saw that Barda had begun to eat, and he did the same. He had never eaten a stranger meal. Not just because the food was different from what he was used to at home, but because it was being eaten so high above the ground, beneath a white moon, on a platform that swayed gently with every breeze. And because a black bird called Kree and a small, furred creature called Filli shared the meal with him.

'How long have you lived here alone, Jasmine?' he asked at last.

'I was seven years old when the Grey Guards came,' the girl answered, licking her fingers and reaching for another fruit. 'They must have come the long way from Del, for the Wenn had not seized them. I was filling the water bags at the stream. My parents were searching for food, and carrying it up to our house in the treetops. The Guards saw them, and caught them, burned the house and took them away.'

'But the Guards did not find you?' asked Barda. 'How was that?'

'My mother looked back to me, and made a sign for me to hide in the ferns and to be silent,' answered Jasmine. 'So I did as I was told. I thought that if I did that, if I was good, my mother and father would come back. But they did not come back.'

Her mouth tightened and turned down at the corners, but she did not cry. Jasmine, thought Lief, had probably not cried for a very long time.

'So you grew up alone, in this Forest?' he asked.

She nodded. 'The good trees and the birds helped me,' she said, as though this was the most normal thing in the world. 'And I remembered things my parents had taught me. I collected what I could from our old house— what had not been burned. I made this nest and slept in it at night, and so was safe from the things that roam the forest floor in the darkness. And so I have lived ever since.'

'That potion you gave us to help us move again,' said Barda, making a face at the memory. 'What was it?'

'My mother made it long ago, from leaves like the ones that grow along the Wenn path,' Jasmine said. 'It cured father, when he was stung. I used it on Filli, too, when I found him caught by the Wenn as a baby. That was how he came to live with me, wasn't it Filli?'

The little creature nibbling berries beside her chattered in agreement. She grinned, but her smile quickly faded as she turned back to Barda and Lief. 'There were only a few drops left when I found you,' she said quietly. 'The bottle is empty, now.'

'Can you not make more?' asked Barda.

She shook her head. 'The Guard's fire killed the leaves that grew here in the Forest. The only others are on the Wenn path.'

So, Lief thought. She is unprotected now. Because of us.

'We are deeply grateful, Jasmine,' he murmured. 'We owe you our lives.'

She shrugged, brushing the last of the fruit stones from her lap.

'And Deltora owes you a great debt,' Barda added. 'For now we can continue our quest.'

Jasmine looked up. 'If your quest to the Forests leads you to the place I think it will, you will not survive in any case,' she said bluntly. 'I might as well have left you to the Wennbar.'

There was a short, unpleasant silence. Then the girl shrugged again. 'But I suppose you will go on, whatever I say,' she sighed, climbing to her feet. 'So I will show you the way. Are you ready?'

14 - The Dark

They travelled through the night, keeping to the treetops, while below them unseen things rustled, growled and hissed. Their path was winding, because Jasmine would only move through certain trees. 'The good trees,' she called them.

Every now and then she would bend her head to the trunk of one such tree and seem to listen. 'They tell me what is ahead,' she said, when Barda asked her about this. 'They warn me of danger.' And when he raised his eyebrows at her in surprise, she stared back at him as though she did not see why he should not believe her.

She told them little about the place to which she was taking them. She said there was little she could tell.

'I only know that it is in the centre of the middle Forest, the smallest one,' she said. 'The birds will not venture into that Forest, but they say that at its heart is an evil, forbidden place. They call this place "The Dark".

It has a terrible Guardian. Those who go there never leave it, and even the trees fear it.'

She turned to Lief, with the ghost of a smile. 'Does it not sound like the place you seek?' she asked.

He nodded, and touched his sword for comfort.

❋

Day was breaking when they crossed a small clearing and entered the middle Forest.

The trees hid all but a few rays of the sun, here, and there was no sound at all. Not a bird called. Not an insect moved. Even the trees and vines through which they climbed were still, as though no breeze dared to disturb the dim, damp air.

Jasmine had begun to move more slowly and carefully. Filli huddled against her neck, his head hidden in her hair. Kree no longer flew ahead, but hopped and fluttered with them from one branch to the next.

'The trees tell us to go back,' Jasmine whispered. 'They say that we will die.'

There was fear in her voice, but she did not stop. Lief and Barda followed her through the thickening Forest, their ears and eyes straining for any sound or sight of danger. Yet there was nothing but green all around them, and the silence was broken only by the sounds of their own movement.

Finally they reached a place where they could go no further. Heavy, twisting vines criss-crossed and tangled together, smothering the huge trees, making a barrier like a huge, living net. The three companions searched to left and to right, and found that the vine net made a full circle, enclosing whatever was inside.

'It is the centre,' breathed Jasmine. She put up her arm to Kree, who flew to her at once.

'We must go down to the ground,' said Barda.

Jasmine shook her head. 'There is terrible danger here,' she murmured. 'The trees are silent, and will not answer me.'

'Perhaps they are dead,' Lief whispered. 'Strangled by the vines.'

Jasmine shook her head again. Her eyes were filled with grief, pity and anger. 'They are not dead. But they are bound. They are prisoners. They are—in torment.'

'Lief, we must go down,' Barda muttered again. Plainly, this talk of trees having feelings made him uncomfortable. He thought Jasmine was more than a little mad. He turned to her. 'We thank you for all you have done for us,' he said politely. 'But you can do no more. We must go on alone.'

Leaving the girl crouching in the treetops, they began to half-climb, half-slide towards the forest floor. Lief looked up once and caught a glimpse of her. She was still watching them, the raven perched on her arm. With her other hand she was stroking Filli, sheltering under her hair.

They slipped lower, lower. And suddenly, Lief felt something that made his heart leap with fearful excitement. The steel Belt, hidden beneath his clothes, was warming, tingling on his skin.

'We are in the right place,' he hissed to Barda. 'One of the gems is nearby. The Belt feels it.'

He saw Barda's lips tighten. He thought he knew what the big man was thinking. If the gem was near, a terrible enemy was near also. How much easier, Barda must be thinking, if he was alone, with no-one else to think about.

'Do not worry about me,' Lief whispered, trying to keep his voice steady and calm. 'Nothing matters but that we seize the gem. If I die in the attempt, it will not be your fault. You must take the Belt from my body and go on alone, as you have always wished.'

Barda glanced at him quickly, and seemed about to reply, but then shut his lips and nodded.

They reached the floor of the forest and sank almost knee-deep in dead leaves. Here it was quite dark, and still there was utter silence. Spider webs frosted the trunks of the trees, and everywhere fungus clustered in ugly lumps. The air was thick with the smell of damp and decay.

Lief and Barda drew their swords and began slowly to move around the vine-walled circle.

The Belt grew warmer around Lief's waist. Warmer, warmer . . . hot! 'Soon . . .' he breathed.

And then, he felt Barda clutch his arm.

Before them was an opening in the wall of vines. And standing in the middle of the opening was a hulking, terrifying figure.

It was a knight. A knight in golden battle armour.

His breastplate glimmered in the dimness. His helmet was crowned with golden horns. He stood, motionless, on guard, a great sword in his hand. Lief drew a sharp breath when he saw what was set into the sword's hilt.

A huge, yellow stone. The topaz.

'WHO GOES THERE?'

Lief and Barda froze as the hollow, echoing voice rang out. The knight had not turned his head, had not moved at all. Yet they knew that it was he who had challenged them. They knew, too, that it was useless to refuse to answer, or to try to hide now.

'We are travellers, from the city of Del,' called Barda. 'Who is it who wants to know?'

'I am Gorl, guardian of this place and owner of its treasure,' said the hollow voice. 'You are trespassers. Go, now, and you may live. Stay, and you will die.'

'It is two against one,' Lief whispered in Barda's ear. 'Surely we can overpower him, if we take him by surprise. We can pretend to leave, and then—'

Gorl's head slowly turned towards them. Through the eye-slit of his helmet they could see only blackness. Lief's spine prickled.

'So, you plot against me,' the voice boomed. 'Very well. The choice is made.'

The armour-clad arm lifted and beckoned, and, to his horror, Lief found himself stumbling forward, as though he was being dragged by an invisible string. Desperately he struggled to hold back, but the force that was pulling him was too strong. He heard Barda cursing as he, too, lurched towards the beckoning arm.

Finally they stood before the knight. He towered above them. 'Thieves! Fools!' he growled. 'You dare to try to steal my treasure. Now you will join the others who have tried, and your bodies will feed my vines, as theirs have done.'

He stepped aside, and Lief stared with fascinated horror through the gap in the vines.

The wall of twisted stems was far thicker than he had realised, made up of hundreds of separate vines locked together. Many, many great trees were held within the vines' net. The wall must have been gradually thickening for centuries, spreading outward from the centre as more and more vines grew, and more and more trees were taken.

High above the ground, the vines reached from treetop to treetop, joining together to form a roof over the small, round space they protected. Only a tiny patch of blue sky could still be seen between the thickening leaves. Only a few beams of sunlight reached down to show dimly what lay inside the circle.

Ringing the walls, overgrown by gnarled roots, were the ancient, crumbling bodies and bones of countless dead—the knight's victims, whose bodies had fed the vines. In the centre of the circle there was a round patch of thick black mud from which rose three glimmering objects that looked like golden arrows.

'What are they?' Lief gasped.

'You know well what they are, thief,' thundered

the knight. 'They are the Lilies of Life, the treasures you have come to steal.'

'We have not come to steal them!' Barda exclaimed.

The knight turned his terrible head to look at him. 'You lie!' he said. 'You want them for yourselves, as I did, long ago. You wish to have their nectar so that you may live forever. But you shall not! I have protected my prize too well.'

He raised his armoured fist. 'When the Lilies bloom at last, and the nectar flows, only I shall drink of it. Then I shall be ruler of all the seven tribes, for no-one will be able to stand against me, and I shall live forever.'

'He is mad,' breathed Barda. 'He speaks as though the seven tribes were never united under Adin. As though the kingdom of Deltora has never existed!'

Lief felt sick. 'I think—I think he came here before that happened,' he whispered back. 'He came here to find these—these Lilies of which he speaks. And they enchanted him. He has been here ever since.'

Gorl lifted his sword. 'Move into the circle,' he ordered. 'I must kill you there, so that your blood will feed the vines.'

Again they found that their legs would not do their will, but only his. They staggered through the gap in the vines. Gorl followed them, raising his sword.

15 - The Lilies of Life

It was dim inside the circle. The golden arrowheads of the budding Lilies were the only glimmer of warm colour. Everything else was dark brown, or dull green.

Lief and Barda stood, helpless, before the knight. They could not move. They could not fight, or run.

Gorl raised his sword higher.

I must prepare for death, Lief thought. But he could only think of the Belt around his waist. If he was killed here, the Belt would lie forgotten with his bones. The gems would never be restored to it. The heir to the throne of Deltora would never be found. The land would remain under the Shadow forever.

It must not be! he thought wildly. But what can I do?

Then he heard Barda begin to speak.

'You wear the armour of a knight, Gorl,' Barda said. 'But you are not a true knight. You do not fight your enemies with honour.'

Are things not bad enough, Barda? thought Lief, in terror. Why do you risk making him even more angry than he is?

But Gorl hesitated, his great sword wavering in his hand. 'I must protect the Lilies of Life,' he said sullenly. 'I knew my destiny the moment I saw their golden nectar dropping from their petals, long ago.'

'But you were not alone when you saw this, were you, Gorl?' Barda demanded, his voice strong and bold. 'You would not have come alone on a quest to the Forests of Silence. You had companions.'

He is trying to turn Gorl's mind from us, Lief thought, suddenly understanding. He hopes that Gorl's hold over us will weaken, if he begins to think of other things.

'Gorl, what happened to your companions?' Barda demanded.

The knight's head jerked aside, as if Barda had dealt him a blow. 'My companions—my two brothers—ran towards the Lilies,' he muttered. 'And . . .'

'And you killed them!'

Gorl's voice rose to a loud, high whine. 'I had to do it!' he wailed. 'I could not share with them! I needed a whole cup of the nectar for myself. They should have known that.'

He lowered his head and began pacing the circle, mumbling to himself. 'While my brothers fought me, trying to save themselves, the Lilies wilted, and the nectar fell to waste in the mud. But I did not despair. The Lilies were mine, and mine alone. All I had to do was wait until they bloomed again.'

Lief's heart leapt as he felt the iron bands of the knight's will loosening, letting him move freely again. Barda's idea was working. Gorl's mind was now far away from them. He glanced at his companion and saw that Barda was reaching for his sword.

Gorl had his back to them now, and was stroking the leaves and stems of the twisting vines with his armoured hand. He seemed almost to have forgotten that anyone was with him. 'As the new buds rose from the mud, I raised my wall around them, to protect them from intruders,' he was muttering. 'I did my work well. Never would the vines have grown so strong without my care.'

Barda made a silent signal to Lief, and together they began to creep towards Gorl, their swords at the ready. They both knew that they would only have one chance. It could not be a fair fight. They had to take the knight by surprise, and kill him, before he could bind them to his will again. Otherwise they were lost, as so many had been lost before them.

Gorl was still talking to himself, stroking the vine leaves. 'I have cut the branches from the trees that dared to resist my vines,' he mumbled. 'I have fed the vines with the bodies of the enemies—man, woman, bird or beast—who dared to approach them. And I have kept my treasures safe. I have waited long for them to bloom. But surely my time has nearly come.'

Barda lunged forward, with a mighty shout. His sword found its mark—the thin, dark gap between the knight's helmet and body armour—and he pushed it home.

But to Lief's horror, the knight did not fall. With a low growl, he turned, pulling Barda's sword from the back of his neck and throwing it aside. And then, as Lief cried out in shock and fear, slashing uselessly at his armour, his metal-clad hand darted out like a striking snake, catching Barda by the neck and forcing him to his knees.

'Die, thief!' he hissed. 'Die slowly!' And he plunged his sword into Barda's chest.

'NO!' Lief shouted. Through a red haze of grief and terror, he saw Gorl pull his sword free and kick Barda to the ground with a grunt of contempt. He saw the big man groaning in agony, his life ebbing away into the roots of the vines. And then he saw Gorl turn to him, and felt the iron grip of the knight's will clamp his very bones.

Frozen to the spot, he waited for death as Gorl raised the bloodstained sword again.

And then . . .

'GORL! GORL!'

From high above them came the cry—as high and wild as a bird's.

Gorl's head jerked backwards as he looked up with a growl of startled fury.

Lief, too, looked up, and with a shock saw that it

was Jasmine who was calling. She was swinging from the very top of one of the great trees, peering down at them through the gap in the roof of vines. Kree hovered above her head, his black wings spread over her head as if to protect her.

'You have made good into evil in this place, with your jealousy and spite, Gorl!' Jasmine shouted. 'You have bound and enslaved the trees and killed the birds— and all to guard something that is not yours!' With her dagger she began slashing at the vines that covered the clearing. Tattered leaves began to fall like green snow.

With a roar of rage Gorl raised his arms. Lief felt his limbs freed as the knight turned all his power upwards— towards the new intruder.

'Run, Lief!' Jasmine shrieked. 'To the centre! Now!'

There was a great cracking, tearing sound from above. Lief leapt for safety, flinging himself into the mud at the centre of the clearing just as the earth behind him shuddered with a mighty crash that echoed like rolling thunder.

For what seemed a long time he lay still, his eyes tightly closed, his head spinning, his heart hammering in his chest. Then at last he became aware of a soft, pattering on his back, and a feeling of warmth. Gasping, he crawled to his knees and turned.

His eyes, so long accustomed to the dimness, squinted against the bright sunlight that poured into the clearing from the open sky above. The roof of vines had been torn through, and leaves and stems still pattered down like rain. Where he and Gorl had stood together only minutes before lay the reason for the damage—a great fallen branch. And beneath the branch was a mass of crushed golden armour.

Lief stared, unable to believe what had happened so suddenly. The Belt grew hot against his skin. He looked down and saw Gorl's sword, lying right in front of him. Almost absent-mindedly, he picked it up. The topaz in the hilt shone clear gold. So, he thought dreamily, the first gem to be found was the topaz—the symbol of faithfulness.

Suddenly his mind cleared. His eyes searched for, and then found, the still, pale figure of Barda, lying at the edge of the clearing. He jumped up and ran to him, kneeling down beside him, calling his name.

Barda did not stir. He still breathed, but very weakly. The terrible wound in his chest was still bleeding. Lief opened the jacket and shirt, tried to clean the wound, tried to stop the blood with his cloak. He had to do something. But he knew it was useless. It was too late.

He barely looked up as Jasmine leapt lightly down beside him. 'Barda is dying,' he said drearily. There was a terrible pain in his chest. A terrible sense of loss and loneliness and waste.

'Lief!' he heard Jasmine gasp. But still he did not move.

'Lief! Look!'

She was pulling at his arm. Reluctantly he raised his head.

Jasmine was staring at the centre of the clearing. Her face was filled with awe. Lief spun around to see what she was looking at.

The Lilies of Life were blooming. The golden arrows that were their buds had opened in the sunlight so long denied them. Now they were golden trumpets, their petals spread joyously, drinking in the light. And from the centre of the trumpets a rich gold nectar was welling, overflowing, pouring in a sweet-smelling stream down to the black mud.

16 - The Topaz

With a cry, Lief threw down the sword and leapt up. He ran to the patch of mud and thrust his cupped hands under the nectar flow. When they were full to the brim he ran back to Barda, pouring the nectar onto the wound in his chest, smearing what was left on his pale lips.

Then he waited breathlessly. One minute passed. Two—

'Perhaps he has gone too far away already,' Jasmine murmured.

'Barda!' Lief begged. 'Come back! Come back!'

The big man's eyelids fluttered. His eyes opened. They were dazed, as though he had been dreaming. 'What—is it?' he mumbled. As colour began to steal back into his cheeks, his hand fumbled towards the wound on his chest. He licked his lips. 'Hurts,' he said.

'But the cut is healing!' Jasmine hissed in wonder.

'See? It is closing of itself! Never have I seen such a thing.'

Overjoyed, Lief saw that indeed the wound was repairing itself. Already it was just a raw, red scar. And as he watched the scar itself began to fade, till it was nothing but a thin white line.

'Barda! You are well!' he shouted.

'Of course I am!' With a grunt, Barda sat up, running his hands through his tangled hair. He stared around, astounded, but quite himself again. 'What happened?' he demanded, climbing to his feet. 'Did I faint? Where is Gorl?'

Lief pointed wordlessly at the crumpled armour beneath the fallen branch. Barda strode over to the branch, frowning.

'This is his armour,' he said, kicking at it. 'But there is no body inside it.'

'I think Gorl's body crumbled to dust long ago,' Lief said. 'All that was left inside that armour shell was darkness and ... will. But once the armour was destroyed, even that will could not survive. It could not survive in the light.'

Barda grimaced with distaste. He looked up. 'So a tree branch fell, and finished him,' he said. 'That was a piece of luck.'

'It was not luck!' exclaimed Jasmine indignantly. 'I told the tallest tree what must be done, and at last it listened. I promised that it and the others would be rid of the vines, if it did what I asked. The sacrifice of one limb was small in return for freedom.'

Barda's eyebrows shot up in disbelief, but Lief put a warning hand on his arm. 'Believe me, what Jasmine says is true,' he said. 'She saved both our lives.'

'*You* saved Barda's life.' Jasmine objected again. 'The sun made the Lilies bloom, and—'

She broke off and turned quickly to look at the Lilies of Life. Lief looked too, and saw that already they were fading. Only a few drops of nectar still dropped from their wilting petals.

Jasmine rapidly pulled at a chain that hung around her neck, bringing out from under her clothes a tiny white jar capped with silver. She ran to the patch of mud and held the jar under the nectar flow so that the last few golden drops dripped into it. Then she watched as the Lilies bent their heads and slowly collapsed into the mud.

'Who knows how long it will be till they bloom again,' she said calmly, when at last she moved back to the others. 'But at least they *will* bloom, because the sun will shine on them after this. And in the meantime, I have at least some of the nectar. It is indeed a great prize.'

'Will you drink of it, and live forever?' asked Lief. But he smiled, for he already knew the answer.

Jasmine tossed her head. 'Only a fool would want such a thing,' she snorted. 'And these few drops would not do the work in any case, according to Gorl. But the nectar will still be useful—as we have proved already today.'

'How?' asked Barda, bewildered.

'It brought you back from the brink of death, as it happens,' Lief murmured. 'I will tell you. But first . . .'

He picked up Gorl's sword. The giant topaz seemed to wink, then fell cleanly from the hilt of the sword into his hand. He laughed joyously as he held it up and the sunbeams lit its yellow surface, turning it to gold.

'What is it?' exclaimed Jasmine. 'Is this what you have been seeking?'

Lief realised, too late, that in his excitement he had betrayed their secret. He saw Barda grimace, then nod slightly. *Tell her a little but not all*, Barda's nod said.

'It is a topaz, symbol of faithfulness.' Lief put the gem into Jasmine's eager hand.

'Some say that a topaz can—' Barda began.

He broke off, startled. The clearing had abruptly dimmed, as though the sun had gone behind a cloud. At the same moment a thick, billowing mist began to form. Kree screeched, Filli chattered nervously. The three companions froze.

Out of the mist, a wavering white figure appeared. It was a woman, sweet-faced and smiling.

'It is a spirit,' breathed Barda. 'The topaz . . .'

The mist swirled. Then there was a voice.

'Jasmine!' the voice called. 'Jasmine, my dearest!'

Lief looked quickly at Jasmine. The girl was standing rigidly, holding the topaz out in front of her. Her face was as white as the mist itself. Her lips moved as she stared at the figure before her. 'Mama!' she breathed. 'Is—is it you? *Can* it be you?'

'Yes, Jasmine. How wonderful it is to be able to speak to you at last. Jasmine—listen to me carefully. I do not have much time. You have done well, very well, since your father and I were taken from you. But now you must do more.'

'What?' Jasmine whispered. 'What, Mama?'

The spirit stretched out her hands. 'The boy Lief and the man Barda are friends, and their quest is just,' she said, her voice as soft as the sighing of the wind. 'It is a quest that will free our land from the Shadow Lord. But they still have much to do, and far to travel. You must join them—leave the Forests and go with them—and help them as much as you are able. It is your destiny. Do you understand?'

'Yes,' Jasmine whispered. 'But Mama—'

'I must leave you, now,' breathed the sighing voice. 'But I will be watching over you, as I always have, Jasmine. And I love you, as I have always done. Be of good heart, my dearest.'

Jasmine stood, motionless, as the mist slowly disappeared. When she turned to Lief and handed the topaz back to him, her eyes were wet with tears. 'What is this magic?' she hissed, almost angrily. 'What is this stone, that it can show my mother to me?'

'It is said that the topaz has the power to bring the living into contact with the spirit world,' Barda said gruffly. 'I did not believe it, but—'

'So, my mother is dead,' Jasmine murmured. 'I

thought it was so—I felt it. But still I hoped . . .' Her lips tightened. Then she took a deep breath, raised her chin and looked at them squarely.

'It seems I am to go with you when you leave here,' she said. 'If you will have me.' She put up her hand to the small, furry creature clinging to her shoulder. 'But I could not leave Filli behind. And Kree goes everywhere I go. That would have to be understood.'

'Of course!' Lief exclaimed. Then, suddenly realising that he was not the only one who had to agree, he glanced quickly at Barda. His heart sank when he saw that Barda was slowly shaking his head. But then Barda spoke.

'I must be growing old,' he sighed. 'Or perhaps I cracked my skull when I fell. Things are moving too fast for me.' Slowly a grin spread over his face. 'But not so fast that I cannot recognise a good idea when I hear one,' he added.

He put his strong hand on Lief's shoulder and turned to Jasmine. 'I did not want Lief with me when we began—I confess it,' he said cheerfully. 'But if he had stayed at home, as I wished, I would by now be dead, and the quest lost. I will not make the mistake a second time. If Fate has decreed that we are to be three, so be it.'

The Belt burned around Lief's waist. He unfastened it, laying it on the ground before him. He crouched over it and fitted the topaz into the first medallion. It slid into place and glowed there, as pure and golden as the nectar of the Lilies of Life, as warm and golden as the sun.

Jasmine stared curiously at the Belt. 'There are seven medallions,' she pointed out. 'Six are still empty.'

'But one is filled,' said Lief with satisfaction.

'The longest journey begins with the first step,' said Barda. 'And the first step we have taken. Whatever the next may bring, we have cause to celebrate now.'

'I am going to celebrate by beginning to rid the trees of these accursed vines,' Lief said, putting his hand to his sword.

But Jasmine smiled. 'There is no need,' she said. 'The word has spread that The Dark is no more.'

She pointed upward and, to his amazement, Lief saw that the vine-shrouded trees were thick with birds. He had not heard them because they were too busy to call or sing. They were gladly tearing at the vines with their beaks and claws, working furiously. And more birds were coming every moment—birds of every kind.

'The beasts are on their way,' Jasmine murmured. 'The little gnawing creatures that like roots and stems. They will be here within the hour and they, too, will relish the vines. In a day or two the trees will be free.'

The three stood for a moment, watching the amazing scene above them. Already some branches were clear of vines. No longer bound and weighed down, they were stretching gladly towards the sky.

'This must have been a beautiful place, once,' Lief said softly.

'And will be again,' Jasmine murmured. 'Because

of you. It was fortunate that you came here.'

Barda grinned. 'I must confess that for a while I doubted it,' he said. 'But all has ended well. Very well.' He stretched his great arms wearily. 'We should stay a day or two, I think. To rest, and eat, and watch the freeing of the trees.'

'And then?' Jasmine asked. 'What then?'

'And then,' Barda said simply, 'we will go on.'

Lief slowly clipped the Belt around his waist once more. His heart was very full. He felt wonder and a kind of triumph when he thought of what had just passed. He felt excitement, eagerness and a thrill of fear at the thought of what was ahead.

But most of all he felt relief, and a deep, deep happiness.

The first gem had been found.

The quest to save Deltora had truly begun.